FREAKY STUFF

Books by Richard Tulloch

WEIRD STUFF
FREAKY STUFF

Richard Tulloch

What slobber Fangs does on his day off... N° 1

Cooking Vegetables

and (plans his evening meal)

FREAKY STUFF

Illustrations by Shane Nagle

Walker & Company ✸ New York

To Will, Alex, and Freya

Text copyright © 2005 by Richard Tulloch
Illustrations copyright © 2005 by Shane Nagle

First published in Australia in 2005 by Random House Australia
Published in the U.S.A. in 2007 by Walker Publishing Company, Inc.
Distributed to the trade by Holtzbrinck Publishers

For information about permission to reproduce selections from this book, write to
Permissions, Walker & Company, 175 Fifth Avenue, New York, New York 10010

Library of Congress Cataloging-in-Publication Data
Tulloch, Richard.
Freaky stuff / Richard Tulloch ; illustrations by Shane Nagle.
p.   cm.
Summary: Brian Hobble wants to be a cool kid instead of dragging his little brother,
Matt, around, but when a television series about zombies takes over Matt's life, Brian
performs the ultimate uncool act to protect him from his obsession.
ISBN-13: 978-0-8027-9623-3 • ISBN-10: 0-8027-9623-0
[1. Television—Fiction. 2. Brothers—Fiction. 3. Zombies—Fiction.]
I. Nagle, Shane, ill. II. Title.
PZ7.T82315Fre 2006   [Fic]—dc22   2006042162

Book design by Jobi Murphy

Visit Walker & Company's Web site at www.walkeryoungreaders.com

Printed in the U.S.A. by Quebecor World Fairfield
10 9 8 7 6 5 4 3 2 1

'B' is for BULLYPROOF?

How to STAND UP to Bullies

A guide by B HOBBLE

look bully directly in the eye

hold lips tight - but don't sulk.

Shoulder pads

WEST ← ① Elbow

EAST → Elbow

grip your hips like you're ready to CRUSH something

① Spread legs apart

FREAKY STUFF

LOOK out, World. Fasten your seat belts. I'm back!

It's me, Brian Hobble, wonder writer, schoolboy hero, class superspunk, and penalty-taker for Garunga Glory soccer team, with another *freaky, weird, amazing, extraordinary, totally unbelievable* (but totally true, I swear) story of things that really happened.

All my friends said I should write another story after they read my last one called *Weird Stuff** (about the pink pen that wrote embarrassing love stories all by itself, remember?). People sent me e-mails, passed me notes in class, nagged me at the bus stop, and grabbed me by the elbow when I was in the cafeteria buying a raspberry drink. That was a stupid thing for that kid to do, by the way. I won't mention your name, but you know who you are, and so does your mom because she had to wash the red stains out of your shirt.

1

The trouble was, I couldn't write another story. I had nothing to tell. It was quiet at our place after Mom and Dad split up. Dad moved into an apartment, and Mom was working extra days. So I couldn't go off and have any hair-raising, spine-chilling, nerve-tingling adventures. Instead I had to stay home and look after my stupid little brother, Matthew. Believe me, spending time with Matthew is normally so totally, utterly, mind-numbingly boring that no one would want to read about it.

Then this *freaky* stuff started happening to me and my little brother. Suddenly I did have another story, even spookier than *Weird Stuff*.* A story full of eerie, uncanny, unearthly, mysterious, ectoplasmic, *freaky events*. You can tell I'm a writer, can't you? I keep a big thesaurus in my bedroom. No, a thesaurus is not a pet dinosaur. It's a thick book with fantastic words in it like "eerie" and "ectoplasmic."

So here we go. In this story I get trapped by a dog as scary as a saber-toothed tiger, I Rollerblade off a ramp 17,000,000,000 miles high, I save my brother from flesh-eating zombies and, most terrifying of all, I kiss a girl. I'm not saying who yet. It's nobody you know. No, I swear, you really don't know her.

Prepare to be freaked.
Very freaked!

* Note 1: If you haven't read *Weird Stuff,* you ought to read it soon, because people think it's pretty good and I do, too, because I wrote it.
* Note 2: If you have read *Weird Stuff,* you know what I mean.

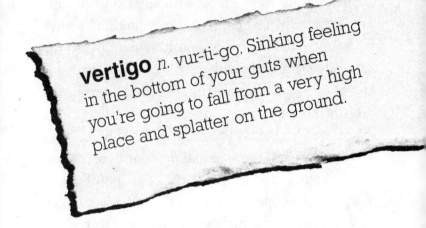

vertigo *n.* vur-ti-go. Sinking feeling in the bottom of your guts when you're going to fall from a very high place and splatter on the ground.

I'M scared of heights. I hate going near the edges of cliffs. I never ride roller coasters. The time Vince Peretti and Sean Peters dared me to go on the Drop of Doom at the Garunga Funfair, I nearly wet myself.

So I wasn't happy, high up in this humongous pear tree, hanging on by my fingernails, trying to reach a stupid orange monkey.

In less than three minutes, either my little brother, Matthew, or I would be dead. If I fell and splattered, it would be me. If by some miracle I came out of this alive, it would be him. I was going to murder Matthew for getting me into this mess.

Matthew had caused all the trouble by (1) going to school with his favorite toy, Funky Monkey; (2) walking home with me, and starting a game of "swing Funky by his tail and see him fly"; and (3) betting me he could throw Funky higher than I could.

I didn't want to lose a bet with any kid who's only five, especially my pathetic little brother. I gave Funky three mighty twirls, sent him soaring into the air, and caught him neatly by his ears. Matthew was impressed. "Wow, great throw, Brian! My turn now."

Little kids are very suspectible to influence (I think "suspectible" is the right word). They always want to copy what we big kids do. Matthew whirled Funky six times and let go. "Look, Brian, now Funky's *really* flying—oops!" The world's first flying monkey crash-landed in the highest tree on the street.

Matthew burst into tears. I put a sympathetic arm around his shoulders and told him that monkeys love being in trees and Funky would be very happy to stay hanging up there forever.

"You're just saying that 'cause you're sc-scared to c-climb up and g-get him," sobbed Matthew.

"'Course I'm not scared," I said. So then I had to prove I wasn't. But I was.

The tree was behind a high brick wall in somebody's front yard. There were no cars in the driveway. The window blinds were all pulled down. The massive chain beside the massive doghouse on the front porch had no massive dog attached to it. Nobody was home.

The big iron gates were padlocked, but there were plenty of curly hooks and handholds, and once I reached the top, it wasn't hard to squeeze between the spikes and drop down on the other side. I was across the patio and over to the tree in no time.

It was easy to climb, at first. There were plenty of low, solid branches. Unfortunately Funky Monkey was stuck higher up, in the crumbling, creaking, moss-covered, scratchy, dangerous stuff.

I stretched out along the last branch that looked as though it would take my weight and clutched it with hands and feet. Funky bobbed just above my nose, dangling at a crazy angle, his tail wedged in a twiggy fork. His pink face grinned stupidly. I reached out my hand to him. Crack! went the branch under me. I grabbed the branch again and froze.

There's this great book, *Zombie Squad Rules*, where a zombie fighter called Storm gets chased over a waterfall by zombie trout fishermen. He clings to a tree sticking out from the cliff and looks down to the rapids far below him. Now I knew how Storm must have felt. Only it was worse for me. It was six squintillion miles from my tree down to the ground, and there was no chance of Storm's gorgeous girlfriend, Mitzi, flying in on an eagle and rescuing me.

Matthew peered up through the gate, offering advice in his squeaky little voice. "You can reach Funky from there, Brian. He's right in front of you, Brian. Brian, just stick out your hand and you'll get him, Brian. No, not that hand, your other one, Brian . . ."

I swear if I ever got down, Matthew was dead meat. If we could rewind this scene and start again,

"A Day in the life of a Zombie"
by B. Hobble

Zombies who look neat, get treats!

[Please do up zipper after lunch is finished...]

"Sometimes zombies get so hungry they could eat a horse...

...or an arm!"

it would be him up the tree and me advising him what to do.

I forced myself to lift my fingers off the creaking branch and reached out my hand toward Funky again. A gust of wind. Funky grinned his silly grin and swayed away from my groping fingers. A brown pear broke free and plummeted down to the patio, splattering with a sickening squelch. The exact same squelch that I would make if I hit the ground.

The wind blew again, this time swinging Funky

back toward me. I grabbed him, stuffed him gratefully into the front of my shirt, and reached my foot back on to a stronger branch. Then my real troubles started . . .

"Ooh, look who's coming, Brian!" squeaked Matthew.

There was a dog at the foot of the tree. A big dog. A big angry guard dog. Judging from the size of his teeth, he was a cross between a wolf and a saber-toothed tiger.

He was snarling. "Rrrrrrrrrrr-rrrrrrrrr!"

Slobber dripped off his fangs, and his stumpy tail wagged. "Rrrrrrrrrrr-rrrrrrrrr!"

"He wants to play with you, Brian," said Matthew.

"He wants to eat me, Matthew."

"He's saying, 'Grrr, grrrr! What's that boy doing up my tree? I wish he'd come down and play with me . . .'"

"Shut up, Matthew."

"Can we go home now, Brian? *Funky Monkey's* starting on TV soon."

I didn't care about missing a TV show about a ridiculous orange monkey. Then I remembered something urgently, vitally, desperately important. Suddenly I knew I had to get out of that tree straight away. If we didn't make it home on time, I wouldn't see the first episode of *Zombie Squad*.

"Rrrrrrrr . . . rrrrrrr . . . growl-owf!!!!"

Pause! Freeze frame!
Hold it right there.

Sorry to have to interrupt this story at such an exciting point, but I have to explain about *Zombie Squad* and why it was urgently, vitally, desperately important that I got to see it. To do that, we'll need to have a flashback.

flashback *n.* flash-bak. When the screen in a film goes wobbly and the story goes back to what happened in the Stone Age or ten years earlier or yesterday afternoon.

I can't make this page go wobbly when I'm writing it, so you'll have to do it yourself. If you wiggle the book around and look at it with your eyes crossed, you'll just about get the right effect.

Then we'll go into a flashback. To some e-mails from about two weeks earlier . . .

e-mail *n.* ee-mayl. Letters you write to someone on the computer and you're not sure whether they get them or not because they don't always write back. Although sometimes they do, which is good because it's sort of like talking to them.

TO: Lancelot_Cummins@lancelotcummins.com
FROM: Brian.Hobble@supernet.com
SUBJECT: Your next book

Dear Lancelot Cummins,

I don't know if you remember me, Brian Hobble. I was in your class when you came to Garunga District School and taught us about writing. I wrote that story about the pink pen that could write by itself and you said it was good.

You remember you gave me your e-mail address and said I could call you Lance? When are you writing a new book, Lance? 'Cause I've read all your other ones, and I think they are the best!!!!

Your fan,

Brian Hobble

TO: Brian.Hobble@supernet.com
FROM: Lancelot_Cummins@lancelotcummins.com
SUBJECT: Re: Your next book

Dear Brian,

Yes, I certainly do remember you. As a matter of fact, meeting you was a great encouragement to me at a time when I was finding writing difficult—it isn't always easy, is it?

Brian, everyone expects me to know something about writing. I've published lots of books. *Brown Gunk from Mars* and *A T-Rex Ate My Homework* have become bestsellers, and rights to the *Zombie Squad* books have been sold to a network for a TV series. However, I was really stuck when I visited your school. I was struggling to write a sequel to *The Haunted Dunny Brush* and was honestly a little bored with it.

But when I learned how my books had inspired you and your friends, my ideas started flowing again. Now I'm delighted to be able to send you an advance copy of my new book, *Nose Job*. (I'll send it to Garunga School because I don't have your home address.) I'd be very interested to hear what you and your classmates think of it.

Meanwhile, you MUST keep on writing yourself, Brian. Your pen story showed what a super imagination you have, and I would love to see more of your work. You have a great talent that shouldn't be wasted.

With best wishes to a fellow author,

Lance Cummins

P.S. Who won that penalty shoot-out and the district soccer final?

Ways I could get famous Nº 1

Become a world class soccer player...

TO: Lancelot_Cummins@lancelotcummins.com
FROM: Brian.Hobble@supernet.com
SUBJECT: Thanks a lot!!!!!!!!!!!!!

Dear Lance,

Thanks heaps for e-mailing me back!

I'm a bit stuck with my writing too just now. I think you got me wrong, Lance. I'm just an average kid, not really a special writer. That pen story worked out well, but it was easy to write because it really happened. I know you think I made it up, Lance, but I swear—*it was totally true!!!*

Maybe if more weird stuff happened to me I could write more, but nothing interesting is going on at school, and after school I just watch TV, look after my brother, Matthew, and make him his favorite sandwiches (honey and peanut butter).

Thanks a lot for sending me *Nose Job*, too. Everyone at school thought it was totally cool that a famous writer sent me a book. You want to know what people thought of it? Here we go, then . . .

My best friend, Vince Peretti, said it was "totally awesome, fantastic, wonderful, and sick."

My other friend, Sean Peters, liked it, too, but you know the bit where the boy sticks the Lego astronaut up his nose to stop it from running? Sean tried that at home and the astronaut's helmet came off and stayed stuck in his nostril for three days.

Cassie Wyman (you remember, that really pretty blond girl who reads loads) said it was the first time she'd read a book about snot, because she's usually not interested in those things. She said *Nose Job* was a cleverly structured story that makes you want to keep turning the pages to see what happens next.

Kelvin Moray said it should have had more violence and blood-sucking vampires in it. (He's a total idiot so ignore what Kelvin says.)

Nathan Lumsdyke, who's a real intellectual nerd,

said he wouldn't actually waste his valuable time reading *Nose Job* because it was actually poo-rile. (I had to guess how to write that word, Lance, so sorry if it's wrong.) Nathan Lumsdyke hasn't read it, so how would he know if it was poo-rile or not?

Our librarian, Ms. Kitto, said good children's literature shouldn't have disgusting green stuff coming out of people's noses. If she bought books like *Nose Job* for the school library, parents would complain and our principal, Mrs. Davenport, would cut her budget.

And you want to know what I thought? Lance, I think *Nose Job* totally kicks butt! Vince and I read it six times (three times each). It's even better than *Escape from Planet Zog* and that was hot, too!

As a writer you rock!!!!!!!!!!!!!!!!!!!!

Signed,

Brian Hobble (your greatest fan)

P.S. About the soccer . . . I beat Kelvin Moray 2–1 in the penalty shoot-out and got to be designated penalty-taker for Garunga Glory. But in the district final we didn't get a penalty. Eastburn Eagles totally pulverized us and won 3–0. I don't want to talk about it anymore.

TO: Brian.Hobble@supernet.com
FROM: Lancelot_Cummins@lancelotcummins.com
SUBJECT: Re: Thanks a lot!!!!!!!!!!!

Dear Brian,

Bad luck about the soccer final. I won't ask about it anymore.

Thank you so much for the helpful feedback on *Nose Job*. I had fun writing it, so it's nice to know that at least some of my readers are enjoying it, too.

And Brian, you are not an "average kid." Nobody is average. Everybody is unique and has great stories to tell. You can write anything at all, Brian. Tell me about looking after your little brother, even if it seems boring to you. Games you play, mischief you get up to, I'd like to hear about it . . . just write!

Best wishes,

Lancelot Cummins

P.S. You may be interested in *Zombie Squad*, starting soon on TV. The series is based on my books, but other writers adapted them for the TV episodes. If you're able to catch it, I'd like to hear what you think of it. Quite frankly, I value your opinion far more than that of any TV critic! The first episode screens tomorrow afternoon at 4:00 p.m.

End of flashback! (Wiggle page and cross eyes again to get the right effect.) Fast forward to me stuck in the tree, Slobber Fangs the guard dog below, and episode one of the Greatest TV Show in the Entire History of the Galaxy starting in thirteen minutes and eight seconds . . .

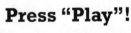 **Press "Play"!**

zombie *n.* zom-bee. Dead person who's been brought back to life by an evil genius and made undead, and now goes around looking for human flesh to eat. (Note: zombies are very hard to kill because they're dead already.)

THE *Zombie Squad* books were fantastic, especially *Z Squad's Great Escape*. I couldn't wait to see the TV show (now starting in just twelve minutes and forty-nine seconds' time). And if I didn't perform a great escape myself, I was going to miss it.

Slobber Fangs looked up at me, his lip curling back to show his teeth. "Rrrrr-rrrrr-rrrrrrrr . . ." (*Meaning, "Come down here right now, kid!"*)

"Shoo—bad dog! Go home!" I said.

"Rrrrrrrrrrrr-rowf!" (*Which meant, "Shut up, kid, I am home!"*)

Matthew called, "Maybe he's a friendly, nice doggie, Brian."

"I don't think so, Matthew."

Twelve minutes and thirty-two seconds left. I ripped a pear off the tree and chucked it at Slobber Fangs. My awesome shot hit him right on the head. Splat!

"Rrrrrrrrrr-rrrr-rowf! ROWF!" (*Translation: Right,*

kid, when I get hold of you, I'll eat you slowly, starting from your toes.)

My chest was tightening up again, so I fumbled for my asthma inhaler. If I was going to get out of this alive, I'd have to enhance my performance a bit. I took a deep puff.

Matthew was making himself comfortable, sitting on the sidewalk outside the gate, preparing to watch his brother get eaten. He was opening his Funky Monkey lunchbox!

"What are you doing, Matthew?"

"I've got to eat my lunch, Brian. Mommy gets mad at me if I bring it home."

Oh, fantastic! I read once that when those ancient Romans went to the Colosseum to watch Christians vs. Lions games, they brought their lunch, too.

Lunch . . . food . . . Brian (the Genius) Hobble has a brilliant idea!

Slobber Fangs turned his head to watch Matthew unwrapping a honey and peanut butter sandwich. It was a totally yucky combination, but Slobber Fangs wouldn't know that.

I edged downward. One foot touched the ground now, but I kept the other poised on the lowest branch, ready to spring back up at a moment's notice. I risked a quick look at my watch. Eleven minutes exactly. If we could distract Slobber Fangs for a moment, it might just give me time to climb back over the gates.

"Matthew, listen carefully," I said. "Wait till I tell you, then throw your lunch to the dog."

"I can't, Brian."

"Why not?"

"'Cause Mommy says I have to eat my lunch all by myself, Brian, and not throw it away or give it to other kids. Or dogs."

"This is an emergency, Matthew."

"I could share it with you, if you like. Mommy won't mind that, because you're my big brother."

He took a bite of the sandwich. Slobber Fangs followed it with his eyes, drooling.

"Matthew-if-you-don't-want-me-to-pound-you-into-little-pieces-you'll-throw-that-sandwich-to-the-dog-and-you'll-throw-it-NOW!"

Matthew lobbed the sandwich into the air. Slobber Fangs jumped for it.

I dashed across the patio and threw myself at the iron gates.

The sandwich sailed to the top of the gate . . . and stuck there, impaled on one of the spikes. Slobber Fangs couldn't reach the sandwich. But he could reach me.

"Rrrrrrrrrrrrrrrrr! Rowf! Rowf! Rrrrrrrrrrrrrrrr!" (*Translation: Great, you little punk, I can reach your leg! First I'll give you a gentle lick to see what you taste like, then we'll get on to the fun stuff . . .*)

I screamed. "Arrrrghhhhhhhhh!" (*Translation: Help!!!!!!!!!!!!!!!!!!!!!!!*)

"Hey, great jump, Brian!" squeaked Matthew. "I never knew you were so good at climbing gates."

I sat on the sidewalk and did a quick assessment of the damage. Scraped left knee, a big scratch across the face of my watch . . . and ten minutes, eighteen seconds before the start of *Zombie Squad*.

"Were you really scared of that dog, Brian?"

I concentrated on picking the biggest gravel bits out of my bloody knee.

"He just wanted to play with you, Brian."

19

Slobber Fangs was pressing his nose through the gate, drool dripping off his tongue. Perhaps he really was a gentle overgrown puppy who was great friends with the family's bunny rabbit, but when a dog's got jaws the size of a steam shovel, you don't take chances. I was glad there were bars between us as I brushed mud off my backside.

"Ooh!" said Matthew. "When Mommy sees how you tore your shirt she'll be really, really, reeeeeally mad, Brian."

"I don't care, Matthew. Let's get home quick."

Matthew sat down and cuddled Funky Monkey, babbling, "I'm sorry I threw you into that tree, Funky. It's lucky we had Brian to get you down, isn't it? Brian's looking after us today, Funky. Mommy will be at her work when we get home, Funky, so Brian will make us some chocolate milk . . ."

I grabbed Matthew's hand and dragged him to his feet and off down the street. Six minutes till *Zombie Squad*. If we missed the show, I'd murder Matthew, slowly and disgustingly. Maybe like in *Nose Job* where Professor Mucus, the evil genius with a really bad cold, drowns his victims in buckets of green nose slime . . .

Five minutes, twenty-two seconds to go.

Matthew was still chattering. "When we get home, we're going to watch you on TV, Funky. And Bippo and Pru will be there, too . . ."

"Sorry, Matthew," I said. "We're not watching *Funky Monkey* today."

"Why not, Brian?"

"Because there's a great new series called *Zombie Squad* that I have to watch."

"Mommy said I could watch *Funky Monkey* while you do your homework."

"Matthew, *Funky Monkey* is the most totally and utterly stupid show that's ever been on TV."

"I like it, Brian. We always watch *Funky Monkey*."

"Exactly. You've already seen enough of *Funky Monkey* to last you till the year 2080."

Excuse me a moment and try not to throw up while I explain about *Funky Monkey*. If you've spent the last eight months living in solitary confinement in an isolation chamber on Planet Zog way across the galaxy, it's possible that you could have missed it. If you've been living on Earth, you've probably already heard far too much about it.

Funky Monkey is this music show for little kids. For totally and utterly stupid little kids like Matthew who've had their brains sucked out by zombies.

An orange monkey called Funky sings songs about putting your hands in the air and wiggling them all about. His friends are Bippo the Hippo and Pru the Gnu, who are people dressed up in animal suits. They all live in a colorful cardboard jungle.

For some weird reason, they are very popular. Shops are full of *Funky Monkey* toys and posters and backpacks and T-shirts, and *Funky Monkey* sneakers tied with *Funky Monkey* laces.

21

Funky Monkey isn't even educational. It doesn't teach kids anything about nature or the real life of monkeys. In a decent wildlife program Funky Monkey would get eaten by Peter the Cheetah, and the world would be a better place if you ask me.

We reached our house. Ninety-eight seconds till *Zombie Squad*. Great! I unlocked the door to let Matthew in, then raced to drop my schoolbag in my room. When I got back to the living room the TV was blaring, and Matthew was singing along with the hideous orange creature. He knew all the words of all the songs.

"I so love a rainy day,

When I can go out to play

Splish-splash, splish-splash go my feet

Raindrops, raindrops are so neat!"

"Splish-splash with Bippo and Pru, everybody," squealed Funky Monkey.

Matthew stomped around the living room, lifting his feet high as if splashing in puddles, making rain-trickling movements with his fingers. Shelves rattled and my soccer trophy (Effort Award—Striker or Midfielder) fell off the mantelpiece.

Twenty-three seconds to go. I grabbed the remote from the sofa.

"*Zombie Squad* will be much better than this," I said. "Lancelot Cummins wrote the stories, and he said I have to watch it. You'll like it, too, Matthew."

"Mommy says I'm not allowed to watch scary shows,"

said Matthew, "and she's the boss in this house."

"Mom's not here, Matthew, so I'm the boss now."

"Can you make me some chocolate milk, Brian?"

"Later."

"And a sandwich, Brian. I'm hungry, Brian, because you made me throw away my lunch. Make me one with peanut butter and banana."

"Later, Matthew, after *Zombie Squad*."

"I'm hungry *now*, Brian. Mommy said I have to eat lunch, and she's the boss in this house, Brian."

"I'm the boss now, Matthew."

I didn't like being the boss. Life hadn't been easy at our place since Dad moved out. Of course I wished Mom and Dad had stayed married, and I hoped they might get back together again. But at least we didn't have to listen to them nagging and bickering all the time. Mom needed to earn more money now, so she was working three days a week and on those days I had to look after Matthew until she came home.

Over the last few weeks, I'd given up a lot to look after Matthew. I couldn't go around to Vince Peretti's to play DeathTrap on his computer. Even worse, while I was babysitting my awful little brother, Cassie Wyman (did I mention that she was The Most Beautiful Girl in the History of the Universe?) was going to the library after school and working on projects with Nathan Lumsdyke.

Three days a week, I had to wait for Matthew at the kindergarten gates with all the moms, then walk home with him. I had to hold his grubby little hand when we crossed the street. I fed him sixty-eight cups of warm chocolate milk, made him ninety-three jam and salami sandwiches, and played Funky Monkey's Happy Families card game three thousand times. I'd even gone down on my knees to find the missing piece of his Bippo the Hippo jigsaw puzzle among the dust bunnies and moldy sandwich crusts under his bed.

Matthew owed me big time now. No way was I letting him come between me and *Zombie Squad*.

The wall clock started chiming four. Matthew made a desperate lunge for the remote, but I ripped it away from him. I wasn't just the boss, I was stronger, too.

I flicked the channel change button. Music

blared. The words *Zombie Squad* slashed across the screen.

Matthew screamed, "Nooooooooooooooooooooo! I'll get nightmares!"

Three teenage kids—Storm, Mitzi, and a fat guy called Big Boy—walked out of the high school gates. Their street clothes split apart, revealing their shiny Z Squad suits underneath.

"When Mommy comes home," said Matthew, "she'll be really, really mad when I tell her what we've been watching."

"You won't tell her anything," I muttered, "because you'll already be dead, since I'll have killed you first."

Matthew tried to drag me into one of the world's all-time most stupid conversations . . .

"You won't kill me, Brian."

"Yes I will, too, Matthew."

"The police will put you in jail if you kill me, Brian."

I raised my fist slowly and held it in front of my face, like Storm does when he meets a zombie in a Lancelot Cummins book. I fixed Matthew with a steady gaze like the one Mitzi uses for hypnotizing tiger sharks. I said powerfully, "We-are-watch-ing-*Zom-bie-Squad*!"

Matthew watched *Zombie Squad*, too.

In an abandoned warehouse, wicked Dr. Overcoat was giving instructions to zombies disguised as a biker gang. "Ha ha, you vill intercept zee oil convoy and pour zee oil into zee river!"

The biker zombies, their eyes dead and red, chanted back, "Pour-oil-into-river." They staggered out of the warehouse and roared off on their motorcycles.

"I don't like them, Brian," said Matthew.

"You're not meant to like them. They're zombies," I said.

"What are zombies, Brian?"

"The undead. They look like ordinary people, but you can tell they're zombies because their clothes are always torn, from when they were killed in horrible accidents. Dr. Overcoat brought them back to life and turned them into his evil servants."

"Who's Dr. Overcoat?" asked Matthew.

"That old guy in the long overcoat and beard," I said.

Dr. Overcoat's face filled the screen, and his evil cackling laugh filled our living room. "Zee oil vill kill everyzing in zee river, hee hee hee hee hee!"

"Why does he want to do that, Brian?"

"Because he's evil, Matthew."

"Why is Dr. Overcoat evil, Brian?"

"He's a bad guy. Bad guys just *are* evil."

"But *why* are bad guys evil, Brian?"

"Because ... um ... shut up and watch, Matthew."

Matthew shut up and watched. At first he rocked back and forth on the sofa, humming Funky Monkey's rainy-day song. Soon he stopped humming. He leaned forward toward the TV, fists clenched. Within three minutes, my little brother became a *Zombie Squad* fan.

Biker zombies overturned a road oil tanker and oil streamed across the road to the river. Z Squad zoomed in riding their animals: an eagle, a rhino, and a dolphin. The fight started. It's funny how zombies look really tough, but when Z Squad hit them they were as soft as those sugary bread rolls around Macho Burgers. Mitzi did three backflips and slammed both feet into a zombie's chest. Two more zombies crept around behind her.

Matthew gasped and yelled at the screen, "Look out, Mitzi!"

Then things got really exciting . . .

Ching-kerching! The sound wasn't coming from the television. It was real. It was right outside the window!

mom *n.* mom. Adult person of female variety who, no matter how old you are, will always love you, make you eat broccoli, and tell you to clean up your room.

IN the *Nose Job* book, this girl called Lisa hears a distant sneeze. Her heart skips a beat, and her stomach sinks to her knees. She just *knows* something bad is going to happen. Then Lisa parts the curtains and sees a tidal wave of slimy green snot sliding down the street toward her house.

When I heard that *ching-kerching!* my heart and stomach skipped and sank, and for good measure the hair prickled on the back of my neck.

The *ching-kerching* was a bicycle bell. Mom was home early!

Don't get me wrong, I really love Mom. Unfortunately she has rather strong ideas about what we should watch on TV. If Mom had her way, she'd superglue the channel buttons to keep the TV tuned to documentaries about the pollution of coral reefs. If Mom caught Matthew and me watching *Zombie Squad* I'd be in more trouble than Lisa when the snot wave crashed through her front door and filled the living room.

Matthew's eyes were glued to the TV. Mitzi cracked her whip, once, twice. She swung it around her head and then slashed out, slicing through a zombie's waist. The zombie's top half looked down in horrified surprise and then toppled to the ground as his legs ran away down the street, with blood spurting up out of them.

I had to change the TV back to *Funky Monkey* or I'd soon be so totally and utterly dead that even Dr. Overcoat wouldn't be able to bring me back to life.

"Quick, where's the remote, Matthew?"

He didn't even glance in my direction. His voice had a strange stiffness to it. "I am watching *Zombie Squad*," he said.

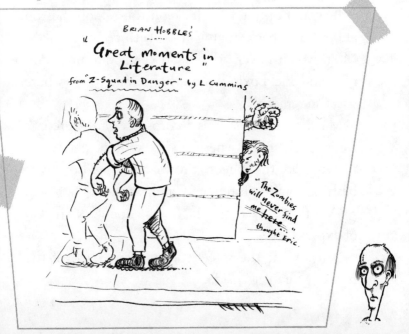

BRIAN HOBBLES'
"Great moments in Literature"
from "Z-Squad in Danger" by L Cummins

"The Zombies will never find me here" thought Eric.

"You can watch *Funky Monkey* now, Matthew."

"Z-Squad-in-dan-ger," chanted Matthew.

A zombie clamped a huge arm around Mitzi's neck and ripped her whip from her hand. Mitzi struggled and kicked. The zombie's red eyes glowed. "Now-you-die, zom-bie-fight-er."

"Never give up, never give in!" Mitzi answered, freeing herself with a judo throw and tossing a can of burning oil over the zombie.

"Matthew, Mom's home! She'll have a total fit if she finds us watching this! Where's the remote?"

I sneaked a look through the crack in the curtains. Mom was wrestling her old rattletrap bicycle up the side path, giving the bell another cheery *chinggg!*

It would only take a flick on the remote button and we'd be back singing along with *Funky Monkey*. Mom would never know we'd been watching zombies and kickboxing and whip slicing. But where was the remote?

Matthew sat as still as a corpse in Dr. Overcoat's freezing chamber, where bodies wait to get reanimated. On the screen Storm and Big Boy were bashing zombies into a gray, pulpy mush.

"Matthew!" No answer. No movement. No flicker of expression.

Bang! went the screen door at the back of the house. Mom was inside.

I frantically tossed cushions off the sofa. My fingers felt the remote, down the back, among the cookie crumbs. That little creep Matthew had hidden it! I aimed it at the set to change the channel . . .

"No!"

Matthew's hand shot out to grip my wrist like a crack of Mitzi's whip. Was I just taken by surprise, or was Matthew suddenly much stronger? I felt as if Big Boy had hold of my arm. I could almost hear bones crack as Matthew twisted. The remote fell from my hand and clattered onto the floor, spilling out its batteries.

"Never give up, never give in!" said Matthew.

Mom walked into the living room. "Brian, Matthew, they let your mom leave early!" she trilled. She sounded so sweet and happy, but I knew it was only a matter of .0000002 of a second and that would change. Her eyes moved to the TV screen.

A zombie, his back ablaze with burning oil, staggered across the street and clambered into the cab of the oil tanker.

"It's all right, Mom," I said, "we're watching this really good show about these superheroes stopping the world being destroyed by evildoers." Mom loves saving the world from evildoers. She works for a conservation magazine called *Green Planet*. They hold demonstrations in rainforests and rescue stranded whales. Storm, Mitzi, and Big Boy would admire Mom's work, but she probably wouldn't feel the same way about theirs.

Storm threw a rock at the zombie's head as the tanker roared past him, crashed into a wall, and exploded in a massive fireball. Mitzi gulped a big breath of air and dived into the water under the burning oil.

Mom took a big gulp of air, too. She knew she'd need it. She was planning to talk for a long time without stopping.

"Brian you know I won't have you watching that violent garbage, and letting Matthew watch it, too, Brian you're responsible for your brother, and I've told you time and time again, Brian, you know we're going through a hard time, and I really need your help here, Matthew, look at me when I'm talking to you . . ."

Matthew didn't seem to even notice her. Mom strode across the room and pulled the plug out of the wall. Z Squad and the zombies vanished.

"Matthew likes *Zombie Squad*, too," I said lamely. "Lancelot Cummins wrote the stories, and he wanted me to watch it."

The spell was broken. Matthew unfroze slowly, turning back into the world's most annoying five-year-old brother.

"It was Brian who put *Zombie Squad* on, Mommy. Not me, Mommy. I was watching *Funky Monkey*, Mommy."

"Is that true, Brian?" said Mom. Her voice was as cold as the liquid polynitrate Dr. Overcoat uses to cryogenically freeze dead bodies.

"Brian said he'd kill me," said Matthew.

"Tattletale!" I yelled.

Now there was no stopping Matthew. He was the world champion tattler. "And on the way home, Mommy, Brian went dress-passing in someone else's yard. And he's not supposed to go in there, Mommy, and he really annoyed their big dog, and he ripped his shirt, Mommy, and he's supposed to be setting a good example for me, isn't he, Mommy? Because we have to help you, Mommy, and be really, really good, don't we? Now that Daddy's not here . . ."

Mom didn't yell. She didn't seem to be angry at all. Her face was as dead as a biker zombie's. Her voice was soft and gentle, like a honey coating on a bar of cold steel.

"Brian, I thought we had a contract. This is a difficult time for all of us and you know I rely on you to look after your little brother. Will you go to your room, please?"

As I edged out of the room, she bit her bottom lip, and for an awful moment I thought she was going to cry.

TO: Lancelot_Cummins@lancelotcummins.com
FROM: Brian.Hobble@supernet.com
SUBJECT: Zombie Squad kicks butt!!!!!!!!!!!!!!

Dear Lance Cummins,

Yesterday after school I watched *Zombie Squad*. I had to miss the end, but I really liked the bit I saw. It was scarier than the books, which were funnier, but I like scary shows. Even my brother, Matthew, was really getting into it, and usually he only likes shows about furry orange monkeys—*you know who I mean!*

Matthew's favorite zombie fighter is Storm, the leader who rides the eagle. I like Mitzi with the dolphin and the whip and the submarine computer. She looks a bit like this girl at our school called Cassie Wyman. Cassie is good at computers, too, but she doesn't wear a blue wet suit. Also, Cassie doesn't slice zombies in half with her whip like Mitzi does.

The zombie fighter called Big Boy is fat and funny, and good at sumo wrestling. I like the way he rides his rhinoceros and eats donuts all the time. And the way he splatters zombies by sitting on them.

Lance, the story was different from the way you wrote it in the book *Z Squad in Danger*. In the book, Z Squad stopped the oil slick spreading by getting all the kids in the town to make a barrier of a million rubber duckies. That was super funny. In the TV

N° ①

Z Squad's Guide to ZOMBIE FIGHTING Techniques

kill 2 zombies with 1 Bird!

show, Z Squad stopped the zombies by kickboxing them. That wasn't so funny, but it was exciting. My friend Vince Peretti thinks we should do kickboxing as a school sport, but our principal, Mrs. Davenport, says she can't afford the insurance.

Your greatest fan!

Brian Hobble

TO: Brian.Hobble@supernet.com

FROM: Lancelot_Cummins@lancelotcummins.com

SUBJECT: Re: Zombie Squad kicks butt!!!!!!!!!!!!!!

Dear Brian,

Thank you very much for your thoughtful comments about *Zombie Squad*. The TV show is different from my books, and I, too, had my doubts about some of the changes the producers suggested. The producers said (1) television audiences like kickboxing and (2) they couldn't afford to buy a million rubber duckies for just one scene. So I didn't get my way.

To tell the truth, Brian, my publishers had to talk me into doing the *Zombie Squad* books, knowing how much young people like monsters and horror. Personally I think there are enough bad things happening in the world without authors inventing even more hideous ones! I tried to make the zombie books funny and imaginative, but it gave me a slightly uneasy feeling to spend my days making up nasty stories, and I was glad to finish the series.

However, boys and girls seem to love the books. Maybe you're less easily disturbed than I am! The TV show, too, has been very popular with trial audiences and I'm glad you're enjoying it.

Now, about your own writing, Brian. I really meant it when I said I wanted to see more of your stories. You said not much was going on in your life, but I'm sure if you just note down the ordinary things that happen each day, you'll start to find incidents that inspire you to exaggerate them a bit and turn them into stories people will want to read.

Just do it, Brian! And show me the results.

Best wishes,

Lance

TO: Lancelot_Cummins@lancelotcummins.com
FROM: Brian.Hobble@supernet.com
SUBJECT: My next story

Dear Lance,

All right, I'll try, but it might be a little boring compared to your stories. Like I said, I don't have much to write about now.

Your friend and fan,

Brian Hobble

P.S. I really like the *Zombie Squad* books and so do my friends, so you shouldn't feel too bad about them, Lance.

buddy n. bu-dee. Person who's supposed to be your friend except you don't like them very much. (See also "buddy movie," where two people who hate each other have to do things like escape from jail and hide from the police while chained together.)

THE next day, something out of the ordinary happened at school. (At least, something more interesting than the normal stuff, like a geography test on the capital cities of South America, turning fractions into percentages, and studying how a blast furnace works—in case we needed to refine some iron at home.)

Mr. Mackington passed sheets of paper around the English classroom. "This afternoon you're going down to the elementary school to work with Kindergarten Green. Each of you will be paired up with one of those little children, and you'll become their 'big buddy.' Big buddies will be responsible for looking after their little buddies and helping them to settle into the school."

Oh no! Matthew was in Kindergarten Green. I already had to spend hours each day responsibly looking after him at home, and now I was supposed to look after a little kid at school, too.

Mr. Mackington went on. "So that they can choose a buddy who has similar interests to them, Kindergarten Green would like each of you to write down a bit about yourselves.

"Tell them about sports you play, or your hobbies, or TV shows or books or music that you like. Keep it simple, because most of Kindergarten Green can't read much yet."

If they're like Matthew, I thought, they won't read anything except picture books about Funky the world's most stupid orange monkey. But no other little kids could possibly be as bad as Matthew. If I was lucky, maybe I'd get a cool little buddy who was into all the things I liked.

I wrote:

Favorite sports— soccer, baseball, World Championship Wrestling on TV (favorite wrestler: Olaf the Ogre).

Favorite TV show— Zombie Squad (by a million zillion miles).

Favorite books— Zombie Squad, or anything else with disgusting, funny, and spooky stories (Lancelot Cummins's ones are the best).

Hobbies—writing (when there's something good to write about ...).

I looked around the rest of the class. Some of these little kids were going to get pretty weird big buddies. Who'd want a big buddy like Nathan Lumsdyke, for instance? I could see over his shoulder that he was writing a whole essay:

Actually as a matter of fact I have many interests, but my passions are actually for classical music, Mozart in particular actually, and reading and writing. I am actually an excellent writer myself, and my mother is actually a published author called Veronica Lovelace. I'm actually already writing my second novel, which is unusual for someone of my age ...

Nathan Lumsdyke was our class brain, but he was also *actually* a complete and utter nerd. I couldn't understand why Cassie Wyman would hang out with him.

Across the room, Cassie was writing a lot, too. I wondered what her interests would be. I knew she liked reading and writing, but what else?

My best friend, Vince Peretti, would put down

most of the same things as me, and so would Sean Peters. Even Kelvin Moray seemed to be writing lots. Kelvin Moray should list his hobbies as showing off and beating people up if he wants to be really honest.

Mr. Mackington got us to put our names on the backs of the paper. Kindergarten Green would choose their buddies without knowing who we were or what we looked like. We'd find out what they looked like after lunch.

Kindergarten Green sat on a brightly colored carpet square and clapped as we filed into their classroom and lined up awkwardly in front of them.

At first I thought they were in costume. Kindergarten kids didn't yet have to wear pus yellow and mud brown Garunga School uniforms. Kindergarten kids could wear what they wanted, and express their personalities.

Matthew wore his Funky Monkey T-shirt, almost completely faded because he put it on day after day. There was a girl dressed as Snow White, and a Spider-Man boy. There was a weird little blond boy with a garland of plastic flowers around his head. He looked vaguely familiar, but I couldn't think from where. There was a boy with socks stuffed in the long sleeves of his shirt to make fake muscles. There were two kids in soccer jerseys. Another girl was a princess.

"This is such a very, very, *very* exciting day for Kindergarten Green," trilled Mrs. Ling. She'd been teaching Kindergarten Green at Garunga since early last century. She'd even been my teacher when I started at school several squintillion years ago. "I'd like us all to say a very, very, *very* special 'good afternoon' to our new big buddies."

Kindergarten Green chanted, "Good after-noon, big bud-dies!"

Mrs. Ling went on. "Our big buddies are going to be our friends, and help us to settle in at Garunga. They know all about the school, so I'm sure they'll have oodles to teach us. Now we're going to pair up with our big buddies."

Pairing up with a buddy was a little like speed

dating, where people looking for girlfriends or boyfriends chat for five minutes to see if they want to spend the rest of their lives together.

One by one, as names were called, little kids paraded across the room to link up with their buddies and talk to them for five minutes. Some started chatting immediately, but most looked pretty embarrassed.

Vince Peretti got the Spider-Man boy named Max. Sofie Poulos and Sarah Griggs and Abby Post were matched with three little girls named Melody, Chloe, and Caitlin. Cassie Wyman got the Snow White girl, whose real name turned out to be Phyllis. Then it was Matthew's turn to get buddied up.

"Matthew Hobble," called Mrs. Ling. "Stand up, sweetie." Mrs. Ling called everybody "sweetie" or "darling" or "sugar" or "gorgeous." Matthew was lots of things, but a 'sweetie' was not one of them. "Matthew, you chose someone special you really wanted for your buddy. Your brother, Brian."

Oh no! My little brother was going to be my little buddy, too? This was one of life's shockingly unlucky coincidences, like the time Storm went hiking in the exact same rainforest that a zombie chopper pilot was spraying with acid.

"I'm sorry, Matthew darling," said Mrs. Ling, "we don't let people choose their brothers as buddies, sugar. You can play with Brian at home, honey, but at school we want you to get to know a new person."

Phew! I sighed with relief, like Storm did when his eagle forced the helicopter to crash into a cliff.

Mrs. Ling continued. "There was another big boy who wrote down that he was interested in almost *exactly* the same things as Brian."

Who liked the same things as me? Vince already had his little Spider-Man buddy. Sean Peters perhaps?

Mrs. Ling said, "We've got a lovely big buddy for Matthew. Kelvin Moray."

Matthew trotted happily across the room and went to stand beside Kelvin. I was floored, flattened, flummoxed, and flabbergasted (*thank you, thesaurus*)! Not only did my worst enemy like the same things as me, but now he was going to be my brother's big buddy?

Well, maybe this could work out okay. Kelvin Moray deserved a little buddy who was an irritating, irksome, inconvenient pest, and it would do Matthew good to have Kelvin as a big buddy. Kelvin was so busy telling everyone how fantastic he was, he'd have no time for his little buddy, except maybe to tease and bully him. After a week or two in Kelvin's company, my brother would look at me with new respect. He'd realize what a great big brother I was and would cheerfully obey my every command.

The buddying-up went on, until everyone had a partner. Except for me. Nobody except for Matthew had chosen me as their big buddy. I was left standing awkwardly at the side of the room, like the girl with glasses in Z *Squad Ball* who nobody asks to dance. (It turns out all right in the book. Storm dances with her and she takes off her glasses, shakes her hair loose, and turns out to be really beautiful.)

That wasn't likely to happen to me. Across the room, my partner was waiting—the last remaining little buddy. I looked at him with horror. Surely that little weirdo couldn't have the slightest thing in common with me?

"Your interests didn't *quite* match up," Mrs. Ling said, "but I'm sure you'll get on famously. Brian Hobble, this is Sebastian Chubb."

Madeline Chubb's brother! Madeline Chubb was the strangest girl in our class. Her backpack seemed to be full of a permanent supply of Nutter Butter cookies. She once came to school wearing fluffy Funky Monkey slippers because her sneakers were in the wash. She had no idea how embarrassing she was.

The Chubbs lived next door to us, and I'd spent the last six years trying to avoid them. I knew now where I'd seen the weird little blond boy with the plastic flowers in his hair. He was Sebastian Chubb, my next-door neighbor and my new little buddy.

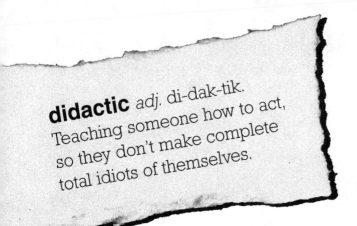

didactic *adj.* di-dak-tik.
Teaching someone how to act,
so they don't make complete
total idiots of themselves.

MRS. Ling said, "Maybe you big buddies could start by telling your little buddies something you remember from when *you* first went to school."

I remembered my first day at school all too well. I wasn't going to tell anyone about it—not even my new little buddy, Sebastian. I hoped everyone would have forgotten what a wuss I'd been when I first arrived at Garunga Elementary School.

That first day, I clutched Dad's hand all the way into the classroom. I was scared of Mrs. Ling, because she wore a dress with eyes on the shoulders. I was scared to open my desk in case I got my fingers stuck in the lid. At recess I couldn't eat my snack because the crusts had turned hard and the peanut butter had soaked into the bread.

Worse, I found all the excitement had made me

really want to, you know, go. Only I didn't know where the bathroom was. I was too embarrassed to ask Mrs. Ling. I just crossed my legs and hung on.

Then Abby Post raised her hand. "Please can I go to the bathroom, miss?"

"Of course you can, precious," said Mrs. Ling.

So you didn't get into trouble for asking! I raised my hand and asked if I could go, too. "Of course you may, Brian honey," cooed Mrs. Ling. It was amazingly easy.

I raced out of the classroom to put my plan into action. I'd follow Abby and she would lead me to the bathroom. I was only five years old, not even halfway through my first day at school, and I was already a genius!

Abby walked down the corridor and around the corner. This was working out so well! She turned left and pushed open a door. I followed her through the door . . . we only have one bathroom at home. How was I to know that at school they have different bathrooms for boys and girls?

Even worse, when we got back to class, it was time for us to tell our news. For news Arthur Neerlander told the class, "I saw Brian go into the girls' bathroom."

No way was I telling that embarrassing story to Sebastian Chubb.

Instead I said, "On our first day at school, Mrs. Ling got us to do coloring.'

"Oh," said Sebastian. He thought for a moment.

Then he asked, "Did you color a fairy, Brian?"

"No," I said. "We colored a picture of an orange."

"Oh," said Sebastian. He looked a bit disappointed. "Did you color with pink pencils?"

"No," I said. "It was an orange, so we colored it orange."

"Oh," said Sebastian. "Coloring fairies pink would have been more interesting."

My new little buddy was obviously as totally weird as his sister.

Next we took our little buddies to the library to read to them. Abby and Sofie and Sarah showed Melody, Chloe, and Caitlin the *Teen Girl* magazines, packed with handy hints on getting boyfriends and choosing the coolest eye shadow.

Kelvin Moray pulled a bundle of *Zombie Squad* magazines out of his bag. He and his friends Arthur Neerlander and Rocco Ferris showed them to Matthew and two other little boys.

I wanted to introduce Sebastian to *Zombie Squad*, too, but I didn't dare ask Kelvin to lend me a magazine. I knew he'd say no, and I didn't want Sebastian to see his big buddy get pushed around when we'd only just met.

Instead I found a book called *A T-Rex Ate My Homework*. All little kids love dinosaurs, I thought. "Lancelot Cummins is a great author," I told Sebastian. "This book's got everything—suspense,

Ways I could get *famous* — No. (2) —

* Ask mum about guitar lessons, or would drums be easier?...

action, teachers getting eaten by monsters. You're going to love this, Sebastian."

"Oh," said Sebastian.

Sebastian settled comfortably into a beanbag chair and adjusted his plastic flowers. I balanced beside him on the edge of the beanbag and read:

"The egg was hatching. Tiny claws ripped through the leathery skin. Spike watched in fascinated horror as a snout appeared. The snout smiled, showing a row of razor-sharp teeth. Ten minutes later a baby T-Rex was taking its first tottering steps around Spike's bedroom, looking for its mother . . . or its prey."

It was really gripping, a fantastic opening to a book. It was exciting, funny, and gross—the stuff normal kids think is great. But Sebastian was bored, even when the baby T-Rex ate Spike's guinea pig. He went to the shelves in the children's section and brought me another book. "Read this one, Brian," he said.

The book was called *Twinkletoes Saves the Day*. It was pink with silver sparkles and had a picture of a pixie with a pointy nose surrounded by flower fairies. Curly purple writing under the title read, "A Fairy Magic book by Veronica Lovelace." I knew exactly who Veronica Lovelace was. She used a flowery pen name when she wrote her books, but really she was Mrs. Lumsdyke—Nathan's mother.

Sebastian snuggled beside me on the chair, curling into the crook of my arm, as I read page one . . .

Twinkletoes was the merriest little pixie in the whole of Wombley Woods.
He giggled from morning till night. He chuckled to himself as he scattered sparkly fairy dust to make the toadstools grow. He laughed and held his sides as he

This was disgusting stuff! But when I stopped reading for a moment to check how many pages of this appalling junk I still had to go (forty-seven, in fact), Sebastian's forehead creased under his flowery garland. He said very seriously, "Brian, did you know pixies like dancing as well as singing?"

"Oh?" I said.

Sebastian jumped out of the beanbag. "Pixies like the music of crickets, frogs, and grasshoppers. They have dancing circles called gallitraps, and they dance like this . . ."

He demonstrated, hopping from leg to leg, knees lifted high. Everybody in the library raised their heads to watch him. Then Sebastian bounced back to the beanbag chair, saying loudly, "Read more fairy books, Brian!"

Vince Peretti and Sean Peters stuck their fists into their mouths and choked back giggles. Cassie Wyman looked up from reading to Phyllis. I hoped she wouldn't think *I'd* chosen the fairy book.

Kelvin Moray imitated Sebastian's squeaky voice. "Read more fairy books, Brian!"

Arthur and Rocco guffawed at this pathetic

attempt at humor, and I was sorry to see that Matthew joined in.

Mrs. Ling moved in quickly. She didn't think Kelvin's jokes were at all funny. "That's quite enough of that, Kelvin," she said. "You get on with your own reading, please."

I read more fairy books, hoping it would keep Sebastian from making a spectacle of us:

Two pretty girl fairies called Peasblossom and Cobweb fluttered in through Twinkletoes's front door. "Twinkletoes, come quickly!" they said. "We need you to scatter fairy dust on our broken fairy teapot." "Ho, ho, ho, not a problem," chuckled friendly little Twinkletoes . . .

Strangely, the more I read this awful stuff, the more I got into it. By page thirty I was really worried that Twinkletoes might not find the missing fairy dust and the tea party might have to be canceled. I was relieved when Twinkletoes remembered he'd lent his fairy dust to a bluebird with a broken wing. He mended the teapot, and all the fairies danced around the pixie in a fairy ring.

When I finished the book, Sebastian's eyes were shining. "Do you think the fairies will leave a bowl of cream on the hearth for Twinkletoes, Brian?"

"Excuse me?" I said.

"Or beer," said Sebastian. "When a pixie helps you,

you have to leave them cream or beer. Otherwise the pixie will come back and put an evil spell on you. Wasn't that a lovely story, Brian?"

"Derrrr!" said Kelvin Moray. He and Arthur and Rocco had been gathered around us, listening to every word. I'd gotten so into my reading that I hadn't noticed them.

"Derrrr!" repeated Matthew. He'd learned his first lesson from his new big buddy.

A distant bell rang to finish the period. As they moved off, Kelvin whispered, "The evil pixies are coming to get you, Brian!"

And Matthew copied him exactly, whispering, "The evil pixies are coming to get you!"

"Matthew," I said. "Wait for me at the gates after school."

"Kelvin wants me to go to his house this afternoon," said Matthew.

"You can't, Matthew!" I said. "I'm responsible for you, Mom says."

"Kelvin's got loads of *Zombie Squad* stuff at his place."

I said, "Matthew, if you promise not to tell Mom, we can watch *Zombie Squad* at home."

"I want to go to Kelvin's," said Matthew.

"You're not going to Kelvin's, Matthew. You're coming with me, and that's that!"

"Tomorrow then?" asked Matthew.

"You'll have to ask Mom," I said. Matthew stuck

out his tongue at me. Then he ran off to join his brand-new, best, most favorite big buddy.

My little buddy, Sebastian, was hugging the Fairy Magic book to his chest. Then he kissed it.

"You really like fairies, don't you, Sebastian?" I asked.

He beckoned me to bend down toward him, put his arms round my neck, and whispered in my ear, "I *am* a fairy."

"Your little buddy is so cute, Brian!" said Cassie Wyman as we walked back to the middle school.

"My little buddy is a complete raving loony," I said.

"He's just a bit different, that's all," said Cassie. "All the girls think he's gorgeous with his blond curls."

"He's got to change," I said. "Kids will give him a hard time if he grows up as weird as his sister."

"Madeline isn't too bad," said Cassie.

"Madeline's so weird, she doesn't even know she's weird."

"Maybe she just doesn't care."

I hadn't thought of it quite like that. Madeline Chubb couldn't open her mouth without someone like Kelvin Moray going "Derrrr!" and encouraging everyone to laugh at her. Any normal human being would hate being teased like that.

"Girls can get away with being a bit strange, Cassie," I said. "If you're a boy you have to fit in."

"Is that so?" she said. A smile curled out the corner of her mouth, like the smile Dr. Overcoat gives when he straps a zombie fighter to his Truth Machine.

"Cassie, you're a girl. You just don't understand how hard it is being a boy. Boys are meant to be tough. If you're scared of something, you shouldn't let anyone know. If you've got a weakness, or you're different, it's best not to show it."

This was turning out to be a strange conversation. I hadn't talked to anyone about these things before. I'd certainly never talk to a boy like this, not even my best friend, Vince. There was something about Cassie Wyman that made me feel she wouldn't make fun of me for saying something stupid.

Yet not so long ago I'd been too scared to talk to her at all. Only a couple of months before, holding a conversation with Cassie Wyman felt like trying to talk with a Macho Burger stuck halfway down my throat.

"Brian, your little buddy's only five," said Cassie. "Don't you think he's a bit young to be learning how to be tough like all the other kids?"

"He's my responsibility," I said. "I'm not going to let him suffer. Not like . . ." I shut up. I'd found something I didn't want to admit to Cassie.

"Like what, Brian?" she asked.

"Nothing," I said. I'd stopped myself just in time, like Storm backing away from zombies on the roof of a forty-story building and suddenly realizing that his heels were hanging over the edge.

One more step and I would have told Cassie the whole horrible story of how people had picked on me when I started at school. I didn't want to be reminded of that, and I certainly didn't want Cassie to know what a pathetic wussy little kid I'd been.

How to avoid Being Bullied N° ①

"Don't wear fairy wings in public!"

"Cass," called Nathan Lumsdyke, before I could say any more, "I've actually had an excellent idea, actually." Nathan was actually always having ideas he thought were excellent, and in my opinion he was far too happy about sharing them with Cassie.

"What excellent idea, Nathan?" said Cassie. Was that tiny smile at the corner of her mouth telling me she thought Nathan's idea would *actually* be stupid?

"Cassie, I've actually said I'd make a picture book for my little buddy," said Nathan, "and I thought I could help you write one for your buddy, Phyllis, if you like."

"That's a very sweet offer, Nathan," said Cassie.

"Actually, we could make them in the library after school today," said Nathan, "or do you actually have other plans?"

"Er, no," said Cassie. My heart stopped beating for a moment, then gave a few extra thumps when she went on. "Maybe Brian wants to come and make a storybook, too. He's such a great writer." She gave me a dazzling smile, the sort that made my guts sink to their knees and beg for mercy. Nathan looked disappointed.

Even if Nathan Lumsdyke was there to keep us company, I couldn't think of anything I'd rather do than spend the afternoon in the library with Cassie Wyman. It was an offer I couldn't possibly refuse.

I refused it.

"I can't today," I said. "I have to look after my little brother."

Nathan smiled again.

Damn, damn, damn, blast, oaths, imprecations, curses, swearwords, profanity, expletives, **&%$#**!!!!

somnambulist *n.* som-nam-bew-list. Person who walks in their sleep, which can lead to accidents so they end up in an ambulance.

TO: Lancelot_Cummins@lancelotcummins.com
FROM: Brian.Hobble@supernet.com
SUBJECT: Something sort of freaky is happening

Dear Lance,

You know how I said nothing much was happening in my life? Well, something *is* happening now. It's weird and sort of scary, and it has to do with *Zombie Squad*, and I think you should know about it.

Yesterday my brother, Matthew, and I watched *Zombie Squad*. I promised Matthew he could watch *Z.S.* to stop him from going to his big buddy Kelvin Moray's house. Mom doesn't know we watch it when she's not home, so please don't mention this if you e-mail me back.

Matthew really, really loves *Zombie Squad*, Lance.

He imagines he's a zombie fighter himself. At breakfast he piles three bowls full of Wheaties, and says in Big Boy's voice, "Zombie fighters must be strong!"

Matthew walks around kickboxing garbage cans, saying, "Never give up, never give in!" like Storm and Mitzi do. Everyone we pass in the street looks at us like we're completely Cocoa Puffs. Matthew can do all the voices, even Dr. Overcoat and the zombies. Yesterday a traffic warden told Matthew off for punching a parking meter. Matthew called in a zombie voice, "Now you die, zom-bie-fight-er!"

Kelvin Moray's been encouraging him. Kelvin's read all your books, Lance, and he's given Matthew the full set of *Zombie Squad* cards, even the really rare one of Big Boy when his rhino was a baby.

Yesterday we saw the episode where the zombies try to destroy Earth by releasing giant mutant cockroaches. Lance, they changed your story again. In the book *Z Squad Get Bugged*, Z Squad open parakeets' cages so they can eat the cockroaches, but on the TV episode Storm and Mitzi just kickboxed the zombies again. I suppose they had to change it because it would be hard to train real birds to eat giant cockroaches. It was an exciting episode anyway, but it had a freaky effect on Matthew.

I have to share a bedroom with Matthew. Lance, that's a bit like sharing with that disgusting Zoggian cyberworm you made up in *Escape from Planet Zog*.

Matthew's mess oozes across the floor like cyberworm slime.

Last night he lay in bed and recited the whole mutant cockroach *Zombie Squad* episode. He knew it all, word for word as far as I could tell, just like he knows the *Funky Monkey* songs. But he's heard the *Funky Monkey* CDs a million times, and he knew the Z Squad story by heart after seeing it just once!

I was trying to concentrate on reading *Nose Job* again, but Matthew's version of *Zombie Squad* went on and on. "Ve vill release ze cockroach eggs in ze city garbage dump," he said in Dr. Overcoat's voice. "When zey breed zey vill be unstoppable! Hee, hee, hee!" Then he did Storm—"Activate the submarine computer, Mitzi! Zombie Squad to the rescue!" And Mitzi, "Right with you, Storm! Big Boy, do you copy?" It was weird how good the voices were.

At last I heard Matthew humming that tune they use at the end of the episode. "Z Squad, dee-da-dum dee daa, Z Squad, dumm-ditty-daa-daa, Zombie Squad, da-da-daaaaaaaaaaaaaaa . . . dee dum!" (Songs look funny when you write them in an e-mail, but you know the one I mean, Lance.)

Then it was quiet. When I raised my head and looked across, Matthew had dozed off, clutching a plastic model of Big Boy on his purple rhinoceros.

I turned out the light, and I slept, too—for a while. When I woke again the numbers on the digital clock were blinking 2:27 a.m.

61

From outside the window, I could hear music. "Z Squad, dee-da-dum dee daa, Z Squad, dumm-ditty-daa-daa . . ." It was very faint, and at first I thought it might be the neighbors, playing a *Zombie Squad* DVD or something—a weird thing to do in the middle of the night, but believe me, we have some weird neighbors on our street. Then I noticed the light from the streetlamp shining in the window. It was giving out this bizarre, eerie, ectoplasmic green glow. And, Lance, it doesn't usually do that. It's normally a friendly orange color.

We sleep with the window open a few inches, but tonight it was wide open and a stiff breeze was making the Funky Monkey curtains flap wildly. I heard a voice, coming from outside. "You won't get away with this, Dr. Overcoat! By the power of Zirgon, Z Squad will get you!" It was closer now, much closer than the music had been. I got out of bed and looked out into the dark.

"This is Storm, calling all Z Squad fighters! Are you ready, Big Boy? Ready for action, Mitzi?" It was coming from our roof!

I slipped my feet into my sneakers, then crept out the back door and around to the side of the house. The bright green light lit up the figure of a little boy, perched on the very point of the roof. Matthew, in his pajamas, was acting out the Z Squad adventure. "Dr. Overcoat and zombies spotted on radar screen," he called into his wristwatch. "Prepare the animal steeds!"

I should explain, Lance, that Matthew's even more afraid of heights than I am. He won't even stand on a chair to get a cup off the kitchen shelf. Now he was up on the ridge of the roof, kickboxing an invisible opponent. "Take that, you Zombie cockroach! We'll teach you not to mess with Z Squad!" He turned an amazing backflip, as good as any Olympic gymnast could do, ending with a flying dropkick into the air.

"Matthew," I yelled. "Come down, you little idiot! You'll kill yourself!" But he gave no sign of hearing me. He ran across the roof ridge, swinging his arms in slashing karate chops— "Pow! Blam! Get a load of this! Zap!"

I needed help. I ran back through the house, into Mom's bedroom. She was fast asleep, arms clutching a pillow tight to her chest, the way she used to hold me when I was little and scared of a thunderstorm. The way she used to hold Dad.

I shook her awake. "Mom! Come quick! Matthew's up on the roof!"

"Matthew's what?" she mumbled.

"He must be having a nightmare. I think he's sleepwalking."

I'll say this for Mom, she's not someone who panics. She's a woman of action. It took her less than three squintillionths of a second to hop out of bed and slip into a robe, as smoothly as Mitzi slips into her blue wet suit.

I led her around the house to where I'd seen

Matthew on the roof. Only Matthew wasn't there. Neither was the music, or the green light. The street lamp had gone back to its normal orange color, shining on the empty roof tiles.

"Brian!" called Mom softly. She was peering through the window of our bedroom. At Matthew, in his bed, fast asleep.

Mom took me back into the house and tucked me into my bed.

"Are you sure you'll be all right, Brian darling? You wouldn't like to come and sleep in my room for a while?"

I nearly said yes. Matthew sometimes ended up in Mom's bed when he went to the bathroom and couldn't find his way back to our room again. I shook my head. "I'll be all right," I mumbled.

"You've had a big week, Brian," said Mom, rubbing a cool hand on my forehead. I loved it when she did that. "You've got a lot on your mind, what with being chased by that dog, meeting your new little buddy, and Dad . . . being away. Try to think of nice things, Brian. Then you won't have any more bad dreams. Good night, darling."

"Good night, Mom."

She left the door open a crack and tiptoed back to her bedroom.

I felt like Big Boy, the time he sees the zombie army marching out of Dr. Overcoat's warehouse. The other zombie fighters say he's dreamed the whole thing, because Big Boy's been drinking lots of red cordial. Big Boy knows that he hasn't been dreaming, and when the zombies set fire to an oil well and pollute a whole city with thick black smoke, he turns out to be right.

I know I didn't dream this, Lance. Mom thinks I had a nightmare. But I know I saw Matthew up on the roof, Lance, acting out a Z Squad episode. It was real. I'm absolutely, positively, definitely, affirmatively, and incontrovertibly sure, Lance. Almost.

Your fan,

Brian Hobble

TO: Brian.Hobble@supernet.com
FROM: Lancelot_Cummins@lancelotcummins.com
SUBJECT: Re: Something sort of freaky is happening

Dear Brian,

I'm so pleased to see you've made up another story. I really enjoyed reading about your brother, Matthew, getting up on the roof. It was clever of you to exaggerate the way little boys sometimes act out scenes from popular TV shows, and you used it as the basis for a very imaginative piece of work.

I liked the way you described your relationship with your mother, too. Very real, warm, and convincing. I look forward to reading more of your family adventures!

I've been surprised at the success of *Zombie*

Squad on TV. It seems that there are lots of children out there like Matthew. Sales of the Z Squad merchandise are really going through the roof. It amazes me that a TV show can have an almost magical influence on young people.

Meanwhile, keep up the good work, Brian—you're writing beautifully!

Lance Cummins

advertising n. ad-ver-ty-zing. Telling people that something will make your life more fun, when really it's a load of baloney. (See also "lies," "fibs," "untruths," etc.)

LANCE Cummins thought I had a great imagination. Mom thought I was cracking up. Matthew was on another planet. I didn't have a clue what was going on.

That weekend I went to stay at Dad's.

It still seemed a bit strange to go to stay with him. Talking to Dad after we hadn't seen each other for a week or so, he sometimes seemed kind of stiff and nervous and asked me things I didn't want to tell him. Mom must have told him about the sleepwalking stuff, because this week's question-and-answer session was more like an interview than a conversation.

"How is school going, Brian?"

Answer: "Okay."

"What's your favorite subject?"

Answer: "Don't really have one."

"Who's the teacher you like the best?"

Liking a teacher? You've got to be kidding!!!

It was like that interrogation in *Zombie Squad in Danger*, when Dr. Overcoat strapped the electrodes of his Truth Machine to Mitzi's brain. (He was trying to discover the secret formula for zombie-repelling suntan lotion, which Mitzi used at the beach.)

"Are you keeping up with your schoolwork all right, Brian?" asked Dad.

"Yes." (*If you don't count being late with my last three assignments. Truth Machine gives me three electric shocks—ooh, ah, ouch!*)

"Because you know we could arrange for you to go for tutoring after school. Would you like that? Or maybe counseling?"

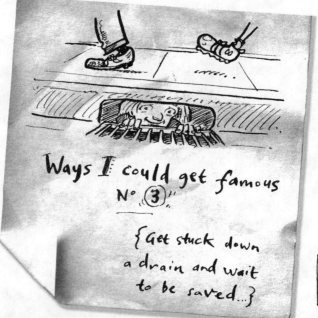

Ways I could get famous
No. ③"

{Get stuck down
a drain and wait
to be saved...}

"No." (*Absolutely true answer!!!! Extra school after real school? Talking to a counselor about my problems? No way! Truth Machine stops bleeping and torturing me. Pain stops. Phew!*)

"Any nice girls in your class, Brian?"

"What? Oh, um, nuh." (*Which means: Ooh-arrgh-umff! You can torture me all you like, I'll never talk! I'll never reveal anything about being desperately, hopelessly in love with Cassie Wyman!*)

"It's okay, you don't have to tell me, Brian," said Dad. "I just want to know you're all right."

"I'm fine, Dad. Don't worry about me."

"Great." Dad grinned. The Truth Machine was switched off at last, and I think Dad was just as relieved about that as I was.

"As a matter of fact, I need your advice, Brian. I've got a small problem at work."

This was better. I liked it when Dad asked my advice. It made me feel sort of grown up. Dad's recently started a new job as marketing manager for Sun River Fruits, a company that makes fruit bars and juices. They're not the world's most exciting products, but it was fun talking to Dad about them.

Dad slid a drink box with a straw on the side across the table. "What do you think of this, Brian?"

I ripped off the plastic straw and stuck it in the box. I sucked. "Orange juice."

"Orange and mango, Brian. Our new 'squeezee pack.' Approved by the departments of health and education. We're selling them in every school cafeteria in the state, so we want kids to like them. Squeezees are one hundred percent juice, with seventeen natural vitamins and trace elements needed for growing bodies. So, Brian, you're a kid. How can we make Squeezees attractive to kids like you?"

"Put a big red label on them, *Adults Only: Not to be sold to persons under 18*."

Dad smiled. "School principals might not like that."

"Dad, kids don't care whether a drink is good for you. We don't even care what it tastes like. It just has to be cool."

"Phew! That's what my marketing team told me, too, Brian," said Dad. "So we're going to market Squeezees with TV ads featuring these really cool kids. I've arranged with Mrs. Davenport to film the ads at Garunga District School."

"Really?"

"We're coming along to the school to audition kids for the roles. We're looking for a super cool, sporty boy to be the Squeezee Kid."

Super cool! Sporty? That was me: Brian Hobble, wonder boy. The Ice Man!

"So how about it, Brian?" asked Dad.

"You want me to star in the TV ad?" I asked.

"I can't say you'll get the part," said Dad, "but there's no harm in you trying out for it. We're hiring a top advertising agency and director. Final casting will be up to them."

Ways I could get famous

Nº ④

{ Get stuck down a drain with a baby whale and have to be rescued while everyone watches TV and hopes we'll be okay ... }

Underground drain ⟶

really dark ⟶

Trying out for a TV ad sounded okay. "Surprise yourself, Brian," said the encouraging side of my brain. "You've discovered you're good at lots of things you didn't know you could do—taking penalties in soccer, writing stories. This is just acting. It's easy."

"But what if you screw up?" said the depressing side of my brain. "You're not exactly the coolest kid in the school."

"You're not a Nathan Lumsdyke–class nerd either," said the encouraging side. "Some girls think you're pretty cute."

"Name one," said the depressing side.

"Um . . ." The encouraging side of my brain wanted to say "Cassie Wyman," but it still wasn't sure what she really thought of me. Although maybe she'd be impressed if I was the cool Squeezee Kid.

"Go on, Brian," said Dad. "It will be fun. It might take your mind off . . . um . . ." He stopped himself suddenly and said, "All you have to do is look good on Rollerblades."

Uh-oh! "Dad, I've never Rollerbladed in my life."

"I know. So here's a bit of an incentive."

He pulled a big plastic bag from the corner and passed it to me. Inside was the greatest incentive I'd ever had in my life. These were the world's smoothest, coolest, state-of-the-art Rollerblades.

"Wow, thanks, Dad!"

"Get a bit of practice before the tryouts."

"Great! When are the tryouts?"

"Thursday."

"You mean, as in, *next* Thursday?"

"You'll be fine, Brian. Kids your age pick up Rollerblading really fast."

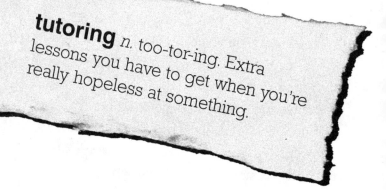

tutoring *n*. too-tor-ing. Extra lessons you have to get when you're really hopeless at something.

"YOU'RE a really bad Rollerblader, Brian."

It hurt to hear someone say it out loud, even though it must have been obvious to anyone watching me for the past hour and a half. I crept along Brownville Road, clutching at every fence and lamppost I could reach. I crashed into stray shopping carts. I put a scratch on the side of Mr. Kettler's new car. (That was his stupid fault for parking it sticking out onto the sidewalk.)

My feet wanted to run away down the street like the bottom half of a zombie sliced up by Mitzi's whip. My legs couldn't wait to escape from the rest of my body.

"I've never seen anyone as bad at it as you are," said the voice again.

I clung to a trash can and hauled myself into a

dignified, upright position. A toxic cloud of Nutter Butter cookie fumes swirled around me, but I already knew who was talking. Nobody else in the entire world could be as tactless and straightforward as Madeline Chubb. She always said the first thing that came into her head. She never worried that people might think she was dumb. Or that what she said might hurt a sensitive person—like me.

Madeline leaned over her front fence, holding out a crumpled packet. "Want a cookie, Brian?"

I hadn't eaten a Nutter Butter since Madeline Chubb stopped being my girlfriend when we were both five years old. Before that I'd eaten loads of them at her dollies' tea parties.

"No thanks, Madeline," I said.

"Want me to show you how to skate, Brian? I will if you want me to."

"These are really special Rollerblades, Madeline," I said. "Dad paid a lot for them, and I can't just lend them to anyone."

"My mom's skates are in our laundry room," said Madeline. "Meet you out back."

The backyard of the Chubbs' house was totally concreted, fence to fence. When Madeline and I were little we used it to act out our superhero minidramas, The Adventures of Amazo Girl and Monster Muscle Man.

I realized that the area around the Chubbs' clothes-line was perfect for learning to skate. Flat, wide, and, most importantly, private. Nobody would see me practicing there except Madeline Chubb. Even if she told everybody how totally hopeless I was, nobody in our class paid any attention to anything she said.

I hobbled down the side path to the Chubbs' back-yard, taking careful little steps to stop the wheels of the Rollerblades turning. My fingers clutched at the spiky bushes growing beside the house. *Ow!*

Madeline was sitting on her back step, strapping roller skates on over her sneakers. They were really old sneakers, with smiley faces painted on the toes. The roller skates were the total opposite of my cool new blades. These were rusty old-style skates, two wheels in front and two on the heels, held on with cracking leather straps.

"Mom got these from my grandma when she was a kid," Madeline said proudly.

Only Madeline Chubb wouldn't be ashamed of wearing those disgusting old skates. No other kid in the universe would dare use skates made sometime back in the Iron Age.

Madeline stood up on the concrete, holding the doorframe to get her balance. Then she pushed off and skated across the concrete toward the clothes-line. Her weight was thrown forward, knees bent. One arm was tucked behind her back, while the other swung back and forth with each step. She spun and skated backward, heels clicking together as she came to a stop under the clothesline.

Madeline Chubb really could skate. I had to admit, she was good!

"Keep your head up when you skate, Brian. Whatever you do, don't look down."

Whatever you do, don't look down. The same advice Mitzi from Z Squad gave to that little boy Eric when she was rescuing him from rock-climbing zombies and they had to cross a rope bridge over the Grand Canyon.

It was easy for Madeline and Mitzi to say. Eric was terrified and couldn't take his eyes off the rope fraying under his feet. I was terrified, too, but I didn't want Madeline Chubb to know that. It was humiliating enough having Madeline teach me something. I hadn't taken her advice since she showed me how to hold a cup at a dollies' tea party. (You hold the handle between your finger and thumb and curl out your little finger, apparently.)

No way was I letting Madeline know I was scared. I'd show her I didn't have a worry in the world and becoming a red-hot Rollerblader would only take a minute for a cool dude like me.

Deep breath in, deep breath out.

Brian Hobble, the Ice Man.

I relaxed my face and curled the left corner of my mouth into a superior smile.

For good measure I tossed my head back and flicked my hair off my eyes with the back of my hand.

"There's no need to look so scared, Brian," said Madeline. (*How could someone whose brain was made of Nutter Butters know things like that?*) "Just pick something at eye level, and skate toward it."

I fixed my eye on something flapping on the clothesline. Go! I pushed off the wall and stood up straight. I didn't crash! I sailed smoothly across the concrete and kept my balance.

Stopping was no problem either. I slid straight into the eye-level thing I'd been aiming for—a pair of oversized underwear waving in the breeze.

"That was better," said Madeline. "Try again."

After a few times back and forth across the yard, holding my head up like Madeline had said, I could skate in a straight line.

"Now hold my hand," said Madeline.

"What?"

The last time I'd held Madeline Chubb's hand had been when we'd been in kindergarten and she'd asked me to marry her. I'd said yes, but I was so young and stupid I didn't know what I was doing, and we split up three weeks later. So the last thing I wanted to do now was hold Madeline Chubb's hand.

I didn't have any choice. She skated smoothly over to me and, before I could escape, she grabbed my hand as she passed. I gripped her arm tightly to balance myself.

Before long we were skating around and around the clothesline, making circles around her backyard.

Cool moves to do on
Rollerblades

By Brian Hobble

N°① The Spin

Hand in hand. It was incredible. After about twenty minutes I could Rollerblade okay! Maybe the Squeezee casting session wouldn't be a total, complete disaster after all.

"You're better now, Brian," said Madeline.

"Thanks, Madeline," I said. "And um . . . thanks for helping me."

"You're not nearly good enough to do a TV commercial, though," said Madeline.

Thanks a lot, Madeline, I thought. Just when I was getting some confidence she has to tell me something like that.

"I could come and hold your hand during the tryouts, Brian."

"I don't think so, Madeline."

I was still holding her hand. I let go and wiped my sweaty palm on my shirt. A bit of a wobble, but I stayed on my feet. With a bit more practice, I found I could keep going around in circles without crashing.

Madeline sat down on the steps to unstrap her skates. She looked a bit disappointed.

"Brian, you'll have to tell the TV people you've only just started skating, and you need a bit of time to get better."

"I don't think you understand, Madeline. I'm supposed to be playing this really cool Rollerblading kid. I'll never get the part if I tell them I've just started blading this week."

"Oh."

"You've helped me loads, Madeline, and I really appreciate it. I'll just have to practice some more before Thursday."

I made another wobbly loop around the yard. Then I stopped. Watching through the screen on the back door was a fairy. A fairy with plastic flowers on his head. A fairy in a torn pink tutu, with ripped bits of cellophane and wire strapped on his back, carrying a stick with a pink star on the end. He was crying.

Madeline threw open the door and cuddled the fairy in her arms. "What's the matter, Sebastian?"

"There was a b-b-bully in the st-street," he sobbed. "He s-said I was a z-zombie. I tried to sprinkle him with f-f-fairy dust, so he kicked me and t-t-tore my wings!"

"Don't worry about that, Sebastian," said Madeline. "I'll make you new fairy wings in Art at school tomorrow." Only weird Madeline Chubb wouldn't be embarrassed about making fairy wings in front of her classmates. "And your big buddy, Brian, will help. Won't you, Brian?"

"*Gulp*, um, sure," I said. I could explain later to Sebastian that sprinkling bullies with fairy dust wasn't usually the best way to deal with them. But something else was bothering me. "Sebastian, did you say this bully called you a zombie?"

"He said I was a z-zombie because my f-f-fairy dress was torn," sobbed Sebastian. "He was a really m-mean b-bully."

Normally I'm scared of bullies. I had bad experiences with them when I was little. Once, Kelvin Moray pushed me really high on the swing and wouldn't let me off, even though I screamed I was going to throw up. I got him back in the end, though. I did throw up. All over Kelvin.

No way was I letting anyone pick on my little buddy. By the time I'd finished with the kid who'd bullied Sebastian, he'd feel like he'd been sat on by Big Boy.

"What did this bully look like?" I asked.

Sebastian stopped crying and stared at me. "You know what he looks like, Brian," he said. "He's your brother, Matthew."

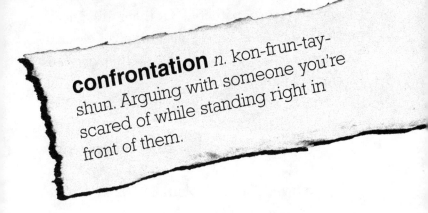

confrontation *n.* kon-frun-tay-shun. Arguing with someone you're scared of while standing right in front of them.

I put my hands on Sebastian's shoulders and looked directly into his eyes, the way Storm does when he's giving advice to little Eric. "It's no good running from people who scare you, Sebastian. Stand up to them and show you're not afraid."

Sebastian put his hands on my shoulders and looked directly into my eyes. "I *am* afraid, Brian."

I took Sebastian's hand and dragged him along the street to our front gate.

"Matthew's only five years old," I said. "We're going to have a talk with him."

Matthew was playing in our yard. He didn't look like a bully, just a really weird little kid. He wore a Z Squad T-shirt, with Mom's wide belt strapping a plastic picnic plate to his middle. He probably thought it looked like Storm's fighting belt.

The costume was pathetic, but there was a fierce, crazy look in his eyes and he talked in a voice exactly like Storm's. "Z Squad will foil your evil plans. Never give up, never give in!"

"Matthew, have you been bullying my little buddy?"

"Zombies must die!" he hissed, and jumped into a karate pose.

"You know Sebastian, Matthew," I said. "He's your next-door neighbor. He's in your class at school. He's not a zombie."

Matthew flexed his little shoulder muscles and stuck his fists on his hips, the way Storm does. Then he pointed to the tattered edge of Sebastian's tutu. "Torn clothes," he said. "The sign of a zombie." He sprang across and ripped the fairy wand from Sebastian's hand. "Your evil cannot defeat the good people of the world, Zombie! By the power of Zirgon, Z Squad will prevail!" He snapped the fairy wand across his knee. Sebastian gasped.

"Matthew, that's enough," I said. "If you want to act out this stupid stuff, that's your problem, but don't hurt little kids like Sebastian, all right?"

Sebastian dragged on my arm. "It doesn't matter, Brian."

I grabbed for the broken wand and tried to rip it out of Matthew's grasp. I couldn't. He clutched it with a deathgrip, like Eric the scared kid clinging to the swinging rope bridge. "You're crazy, Matthew!" I yelled. He turned to face me, breathing heavily. "Matthew," I said, "if this is a sick game, stop it now. Or is there really something wrong with you? Do you need help?"

Surprisingly, Sebastian stepped over and stroked Matthew's shoulder. "I could be your fairy companion, Matthew. Sick children need a fairy to keep them safe when danger threatens."

Matthew swung back his fist and for a moment I thought he was going to smash it into Sebastian's face—

"Greetings, little buddy!" called Kelvin Moray. Kelvin Moray was the last person I needed around at the moment. When you're trying to stop your little brother from becoming a violent zombie basher, you don't want him mixing with the worst thug in Garunga.

Matthew seemed very pleased to see Kelvin. "Greetings, Z Squad Controller!" he called. Kelvin and Matthew gave each other Z Squad salutes, placing clenched fists over their hearts.

"What do you want, Kelvin?" I asked.

"Just brought something for Matty," said Kelvin.

"Kelvin," I said, "Matthew's not well at the moment."

"What's wrong with him?" asked Kelvin.

"I have the power of Zirgon!" called Matthew. "Never give up, never give in!"

Kelvin laughed. "Fantastic, Storm!"

85

I drew Kelvin aside. "Kelvin, something weird is going on here."

"Your brother's a real cool little kid, Brian. It's too bad being cool doesn't run in the family."

"Kelvin, I don't think it's a good idea for Matthew to hang around with you. He's got this really freaky thing about *Zombie Squad*."

"So? Lots of kids like *Zombie Squad*. It's a cool show."

"But Matthew's acting it out all the time. Do you want your little buddy to be a total Cocoa Puff?"

Kelvin grinned. He pulled something from his pocket and tossed it to Matthew. "Here, Matty, see if this fits you."

It was a striped headband with a Z Squad badge, like the one Storm wears. Matthew pulled on the headband and sprang into a karate pose. "Take that, zombie!" He threw a high kick at the potted palm on the veranda, sending it flying. "Pow!"

Kelvin laughed. "He's really good, isn't he? Hey, Matty, I've got Z Squad on DVD now. Can you come around to my house tomorrow?"

"No, he can't," I said.

Matthew crossed his fists on his chest. "By the power of Zirgon, I will be there. Never give up, never give in!"

"See you after school then," said Kelvin.

"Kelvin, this is seriously freaky. It's dangerous to get Matthew into *Zombie Squad*."

"Derrrr, Brian! You think it's too violent for little kids? Man, it's just a TV show. Lighten up."

I pulled Sebastian toward me and spun him around to show Kelvin the broken wings.

"Matthew did this. He's been bullying my little buddy."

"Your little buddy's weird," Kelvin snorted, poking a finger into Sebastian's chest.

Z Squad's Guide to ZombiE fighting TECHNIQUES No. 3

Razor-thin zombie cutting whip
SLICE
"The HORIZONTAL Slice"

Matthew poked his finger into Sebastian's chest, too. "Zombie!"

"If you go around dressed as a fairy you're asking for it, aren't you?" sneered Kelvin.

Sebastian turned to blink up at me. "What am I asking for, Brian?"

"Just ignore them, Sebastian," I said. "They're being stupid."

"Not as stupid as you, Brian," said Kelvin. "You only got that weird little buddy 'cause no one else wanted you. See you, Matty."

"Farewell," said Matthew, in a perfect imitation of Storm's voice. "May the power of Zirgon go with you."

Kelvin sauntered off. (Note the way I used another good thesaurus word—"sauntered" means he walked in a really casual way, like he thought he was really cool and didn't care what I said to him.)

Matthew propped the palm up again and kicked it over once more. "How do you like that, Zombie?"

Sebastian watched for a moment. His little face was dead straight and his voice was totally serious. "Should I put a spell on him, Brian? I've still got some sparkly fairy dust in my pocket."

"Not just now, Sebastian," I said. "But it's very nice of you to offer to help."

reflection n. ree-flek-shun. Bit in the middle of a story where you think about the mess you're getting into and wonder how you're ever going to get out of it. (Note: you can do reflection looking at yourself in the mirror, or in the shower, or by making a list on paper. Warning note: don't try making a reflection list on paper while in the shower.)

THINGS THAT HAVE GONE WRONG SO FAR

by B. Hobble

1) My brother has gone nuts and his big buddy is a complete idiot

This is a problem because:

(a) Mom expects me to look after him

(b) People will think I'm nuts too if I've got a brother who believes he's a zombie fighter

(c) I don't want Matthew to like Kelvin Moray more than he likes me

Action required:

Can't think of any action I could do at the moment.

2) My parents think I need help

This is a problem because:

(a) I don't want to worry them when they've got enough worries of their own

(b) I don't want to go to counseling or get put in an institution for kids who have nightmares about Z Squad

<u>Action required:</u>

Try to appear as normal and happy as possible.

3) A nerd is taking my potential girlfriend to the library and making picture books with her

This is a problem because:

(a) I sort of like Cassie Wyman. A lot.

(b) I can't stand Nathan Lumsdyke

(c) I don't want her to like him more than she likes me

<u>Action required:</u>

(a) press fire alarm to have library evacuated after school (probably not a great idea — might work once but people would get suspicious if I kept on doing it)

(b) do something cool and awesome to show Cassie I'm better than Nathan

(can't think just now what that cool and awesome thing could be)

4) My little buddy thinks he's a fairy

This is a problem because:

(a) Sebastian isn't just a weird kid, he's pretty amazing.

Any normal kid would try to escape from a bully, but Sebastian wants to look after Matthew and be his fairy companion. He's the only person in the world apart from me who knows that bullies have problems, too, and Matthew needs help.

(b) If Sebastian keeps up this fairy stuff, every bully in the world will make his life miserable. I don't want him to get picked on like I was when I first went to school.

Action required:

Bully-proof Sebastian by:

(a) stopping him from wearing wings in public

(b) teaching him to do karate, kick-boting, or all-in knuckle-duster fighting

(Sub-problem — I don't know how to do those self-defense things myself)

(Sub-thought: Sean Peters's big sister did self-defense classes where you learn to walk in the street holding your shoulders back. She taught Sean how to give people a "don't mess with me" look right in the eye and stick out your chin. But when Sean showed me The Look, it made me want to whack him on his stuck-out chin, so I don't think this would work with Sebastian.)

Alternative bully-proofing action could be:

(c) teach Sebastian to be good at sports. Give him cricket lessons.

5) My Rollerblading is pathetic

This is a problem because:

(a) the Squeezee ad casting session is on Thursday

(b) it's at our school so everyone will be watching

(c) everyone might include Cassie Wyman

Action required:

(a) practice Rollerblading

(b) hope the school gets destroyed by an earth-quake before Thursday

Bad places to land on Rollerblades

N° 1

➡ Your mom's favorite flower garden...

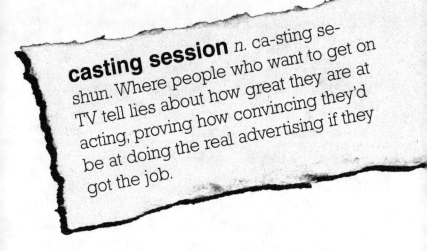

casting session n. ca-sting se-shun. Where people who want to get on TV tell lies about how great they are at acting, proving how convincing they'd be at doing the real advertising if they got the job.

THERE was no earthquake. On Thursday there was a sign up outside the school office:

SQUEEZEE AUDITIONS—
FOLLOW THE ARROWS.

Vince, Sean, and I followed the arrows down the corridors, our Rollerblades slung over our shoulders.

"Coming through, losers!" yelled a voice behind me.

A heavy figure thumped into my shoulder, spinning me around and almost knocking me over. Kelvin Moray and Rocco Ferris whipped past us on their Rollerblades. Kelvin wheeled expertly to a stop in front of me. He was good. "Cool blades, Brian," he sneered. "Are they new?"

"Don't look like you've used them much," added Rocco.

"Or ever!" snorted Kelvin. He jerked his head toward the ramp leading down to the playground, and he and Rocco bladed smoothly away.

"Don't worry about him, Brian," said Sean. "In films they have these trick special effects to make it seem like you're better at skating than you really are."

Sean Peters was an expert on everything and loved sharing his inside knowledge with anyone who'd listen. Vince and I were his only friends, so it was usually us who did the listening. "You'll get the Squeezee Kid part if you've got The Look," said Sean.

"What's The Look?" I asked.

"The Look is what makes you a star," said Sean. "They always have a Look in mind when they cast people to be in a film. Even if you're hopeless at Rollerblading, they cast you if you've got The Look."

Speaking of The Look, who should come around the corner but Cassie Wyman. In my opinion Cassie Wyman had The Look more than any film star in the entire history of cinema. She said, "I think it's unfair that only boys can try out for the commercial. There must be girls at this school who can skate well enough."

The whiff of Nutter Butters crept up and hit me from behind. "They've already got a girl," said Madeline Chubb. "She's prettier than us."

I thought of saying gallantly that nobody in the galaxy was prettier than Cassie, but that wasn't something I could say in front of Vince and Sean. I didn't want it spread around the whole school that I thought Cassie Wyman was cute.

Madeline pointed down to the flat asphalt area between the drinking fountains and the main building. They certainly did have a girl. She came very close to being prettier than Cassie. The girl was super fantastically unbelievably drop-dead gorgeous. And she knew it.

She had a small ramp and two garbage bins set up on the asphalt area by the drinking fountains, and was Rollerblading in figure-eights, whizzing around and between them. A dark ponytail licked out from under her silver crash helmet, flicking like Mitzi's whip each time she changed direction. Tight pink top, bare midriff, perfectly toned legs in silver stockings, cool black kneepads.

There was a gaggle of senior boys clustered around, nudging each other and whispering as they watched her. Even they didn't dare whistle or call out to such a goddess.

She knew the boys were there, but she pretended not to notice, eyes hidden behind expensive sunglasses, making elegant sweeps and turns, her silver butt stuck out behind.

As we approached she went scooping up the ramp, caught the rail, and paused for breath at the top, wiping the merest bead of sweat from her cheek. She glanced at us for a moment, then flipped her shades up onto her head and pretended to adjust her wrist guards.

"Oh wow," said Vince, scratching the back of his head, "she is so hot!"

"Girls are more natural Rollerbladers than guys," said Sean Peters. "I saw it on this TV show *Cool Blades*. Girls have better balance, like when they do gymnastics they're really good at the beams and floor work . . ." We called Sean Peters Seven Eleven, because he had a mouth like an all-night store, which never closes. Our sports teacher, Mr. Quale, said Sean would be able to talk under wet concrete. "Guys have more raw muscle power," said Sean, "so we can get out of trouble more easily if we lose our balance . . ."

He was still talking as we filed into the classroom at the foot of the stairs.

It had been set up like a sort of waiting room, with kids sitting on chairs around the edge. At the desk in front, a lady with a clipboard was deep in conversation with two men. One wore a leather jacket and Yankees baseball cap and had a video camera over his shoulder. I knew the other man, the one in a suit. He was my dad. When I caught his eye he gave me a secret wink that no one else could see. Everyone saw it.

"Why is that guy giving Brian a secret wink?" Rocco Ferris asked Kelvin.

"Derrrr! That's Brian's dad," said Vince. "Ow! What did you kick me for, Brian?"

We Garunga kids all looked very unglamorous next to the kids from other schools. We were still in our yuck brown and diarrhea yellow uniforms. The other kids wore a variety of cool baggy pants and bomber jackets.

"And what's your name, darling?" asked the lady with the clipboard.

"Brian Hobble," I said.

"Oh, Brian, of course." She, too, gave me a secret wink. "I'm Lisa, the production assistant. Do you have any TV acting experience, darling?"

Sean Peters had a video camera at his place and we once made a gangster movie with water pistols and tomato sauce for blood. I didn't think being shot against Sean Peters's garage door counted as "TV acting experience."

"No experience," I said.

Lisa was about to write this on her clipboard, but Dad quickly butted in. "He's just being modest. Brian's starred in several school plays."

I'd been in two school plays. I certainly hadn't been the star. My roles so far had been (1) a talking rock in the Kindergarten Green production of *Little Red Riding Hood* and (2) Lost Boy 3 in Year Four's version of *Peter Pan*.

So far in my entire glittering stage career, I'd had a grand total of two lines.

Talking Rock had said, "Sit on me and rest a while, Little Red Riding Hood."

Lost Boy 3 had called, "Look out, Peter Pan, here come the pirates!"

Lisa wrote down "stage actor."

Other boys in the room seemed to know each other. They chatted about roles they'd had. "Hi, Justin, haven't seen you since we did the Chicky Chips commercial."

"I've had a major role in *Bayside Hospital*, playing a shark attack victim. I had three scenes with Nicole Bussel. She said I was the most mature actor of my age she'd ever worked with."

I recognized the boy next to me, who was telling Justin, "I've just done a call-back audition for that new feature film *Desert Rats*. The director told my agent he really loved my work as the deaf boy's best friend in *Silent World*. And of course you would've seen me in the ads for Holland Cookies, Medical Benefit Society, Zapper Laser Guns, and Buffo."

That was where I'd seen him before. He was the kid in the Buffo dog-food ad, who hugs his poodle and says, "Buffo is best for Biffo."

"What parts have you played?" the Buffo boy asked me.

I didn't want to tell him about Talking Rock and Lost Boy 3. I've got this trick I can do of raising one eyebrow and crinkling my forehead, and curling the corner of my mouth at the same time. It looks exactly like the inscrutable smile of an evil Japanese warlord and makes me seem really dark and mysterious.

I did the smile, and I added a little glance at the floor to make myself look modest as well. If she'd seen my brilliant bit of acting, Nicole Bussel would have had a rethink about who was the most mature actor of my age. "There's something very big coming up," I said, "but the producers won't release the details until the press launch."

"Wow!" said the Buffo boy.

Clipboard Lisa had finished taking names. She clapped her hands to get silence. "Now, darlings, please come out to the playground, and we'll see you on the Rollerblades." Uh-oh. This was it!

On the asphalt near the water fountains, the area around the ramp had been cordoned off with the sort of plastic ribbons you see on police shows where they don't want the public to go near the dead bodies until the detectives have photographed them. There were no bodies at this crime scene yet, but I knew that once I started Rollerblading my body could be lying there very soon, getting chalk marks drawn around it.

A cameraman was aiming a video camera on a tripod at the ramp. Talking to the cameraman was the guy in the Yankees baseball cap. Clipboard Lisa clapped her hands again. "Darlings, I'd like to introduce you to our director, Rob Bridey."

"Thanks, Lisa," said Rob Bridey, the Yankees fan. "Okay, guys, listen up here. We're gonna shoot the blading stuff now, to see what you dudes are

Bad Places to land in Rollerblades

Nº 2 : Compost heap full of worms

made of. Do some cool tricks on those blades, guys. Now's the time to pull out all the stops!"

The cute girl on the blades rolled over to Lisa.

"And, darlings," said Lisa, "this is Tiffany."

Tiffany gave us one of those waves where you just hold up one hand and waggle the fingers a bit. Cute girls must practice that wave in front of the mirror for hours. They can all do it really well.

Rob Bridey tipped his baseball cap back and tucked his thumbs into his belt. "Guys, when I say 'action,' I want to see you dudes skate down the ramp, weaving through the drink packs and doing your tricks. Scoop up the last pack, hold it out to Tiffany, and say, 'Like a Squeezee?' Tiffany says, 'Yes pleasee,' and that's it. Let's see it, guys."

It sounded so simple. Except maybe the skating down the ramp, the weaving, and the drink-pack scooping. That would be really hard for a hopeless Rollerblader like me. If I survived the skating I could probably manage to say "Like a Squeezee?" all right. Although maybe it would be harder to say it to Tiffany. Talking to cute girls always makes me nervous.

Kids from the other schools went first. They rolled and weaved and scooped. Over and over the lines were repeated: "Like a Squeezee?" "Yes pleasee."

After each kid, Clipboard Lisa called, "Thank you, darling. Next."

Then it was the turn of the Garunga kids. Kelvin Moray skated neatly off the ramp and weaved through the drink packs twice. He was such a show-off. When he asked the lovely Tiffany "Like a Squeezee?" did she say "Yes, pleasee" a bit more enthusiastically than she'd done with other kids? Kelvin wheeled around and smirked like an Olympic skier who's just registered the best time in the Giant Slalom.

Vince and Rocco could skate pretty well, but both of them looked a bit awkward scooping up the last drink pack. Rocco fluffed his lines and asked Tiffany, "Like a Pleasee?"

Sean Peters didn't make it past the ramp. His legs went from under him and he sat down hard on the top, banging his helmet against the railing. Kelvin and Rocco burst out laughing and Kelvin called, "Derrrr!"

"Cut!" called Rob Bridey, glaring at Kelvin.

"That's all we need to see today, Sean darling," called Lisa. "Are you all right? Just give it a rub, dear. Next."

Next was me. I tottered toward the ramp, trying not to let my Rollerblades actually roll. I grabbed the handrail and hauled myself up the ramp. Sean had already unclipped his blades and was tiptoeing off the ramp in his socks.

"Good luck, Brian," he said. "How do you think I went, by the way?"

"You had The Look, Sean," I said.

"Really?" said Sean, cheering up. "I thought I might have come across as a bit nervous."

"No one would have noticed," I said.

Then I turned to the camera, teetering on the top of the ramp, clutching the rail with white knuckles. It was only three feet high. But with the Rollerblades about to slide away underneath me I felt like Mitzi the time the zombies forced her to the edge of Niagara Falls.

Everyone was watching me: Dad, Vince and Sean, Kelvin and Rocco, Madeline Chubb, even Cassie Wyman. This could be my chance to do the cool, brilliant, impressive thing, but somehow I knew that wasn't going to happen.

Out on the asphalt, the gorgeous Tiffany was sweeping around in circles. "Action!" called Rob Bridey. Deep breath in, deep breath out. Go!

My knees buckled. My arms flailed like the blades of some bizarre windmill. My feet couldn't wait to get to the bottom of the ramp, so the top half of me had to throw itself forward to catch up. Then we hit the flat ground and zoomed toward the row of Squeezee packs. No way could I zigzag between them. I was totally out of control.

One time in *Zombie Squad*, Big Boy got stuck on the roof of a runaway truck full of toxic chemical sludge. As the sludge truck rumbled through the city smashing into things, Big Boy steered with his feet and swung his arms like fan blades to punch out the zombies who were attacking him from all sides.

I swung my arms like fan blades, too, but I was just trying to keep my balance. I slid straight past the first three Squeezee packs. From the corner of my eye I saw Tiffany skating toward me at a million miles an hour. We were on a direct collision course!

I shut my eyes. My feet headed upward as the rest of me headed downward. I landed on my backside. There was a massive explosion, with something sickeningly squelchy about the sound.

I could feel something cool and sticky spreading up through my pants. I opened my eyes. Instead of scooping up the last Squeezee pack, I'd sat down on it, flattened it, and squirted Squeezee juice everywhere.

Most of the juice had hit Tiffany full in the face. For a moment, this ever-so-confident girl seemed unsure what to do. Thick orange Squeezee juice dribbled down the smooth sunglasses, dripped in thick globs onto her top, and slid down toward her bare midriff.

I pulled the crumpled wreckage of the drink pack from under my bottom. I held it up to her. "Like a Squeezee?" I said.

"Er, I don't think so," said Tiffany.

"Cut!" called Rob Bridey.

Vince and Sean were rolling on the ground laughing. Cassie Wyman was looking thoughtful. Kelvin and Rocco were hooting and "derrrring" furiously. Dad was deep in serious conversation with Clipboard Lisa.

Lisa broke away and clapped her hands for attention. "Darlings, you were all just lovely. Now back into the classroom for just a few more minutes . . ."

"We could be lucky, Brian," said Sean. "We might have had The Look."

"We had The Look all right, Sean. The Look of complete and utter dorks!"

"Maybe it's for the best," said Vince. "Kids who become child film stars get their lives ruined. Like, look at that kid Chadley Stevens. He was a millionaire when he was nine years old, because he starred in that film *Like Father, Like Son*. Then, not long after, he gets arrested for shoplifting a pack of bubblegum. We just had a lucky escape, Brian. Becoming the Squeezee Kid would only have made us miserable."

It was all Dad's fault. He should never have pushed me into this junk. I knew I couldn't Rollerblade for nuts. Why do parents always try to make you do things you don't want to do? Not every kid is going to be a great concert pianist, no matter how much music practice they're forced to do. Why couldn't Dad accept that I wasn't ever going to skate well enough to become the Squeezee Kid? The audition had made me a laughingstock in front of my friends and totally ruined my chances of impressing Cassie.

Clipboard Lisa came in again. "Darlings, it's been lovely of you to come and try out, and Mr. Hobble from the Squeezee people has been very pleased with the work you've done." Dad patted his hands together, giving everyone a little clap of congratulations. "Unfortunately we can't make you all the Squeezee Kids, but we'll keep your names on file, and if anything comes up later we'll be sure to let you know. But," she ran her finger down the clipboard, "Kelvin Moray, could you wait behind for a moment?"

"Sure," said Kelvin. He looked around the room, smiling the smug, smirky, smarmy, self-satisfied smile Dr. Overcoat gives when his zombies have just sucked out someone's liver.

Lisa was looking at her clipboard again. "And where's . . . Brian Hobble?"

I raised my hand.

"Here, miss."

"Congratulations, Brian, darling," said Lisa. "We're all really looking forward to working with you. You're going to be the new Squeezee Kid."

Reply to a Valentine from someone you didn't want to get a Valentine from in the first place . . .

Violets are Blue
Roses are Red
If you think I love you
You're sick in the head

nepotism *n.* ne-po-tiz-um. When you get a job because your dad's the boss, and you're pretty sure you'll screw up when you have to do the work.

KIDS at school were as surprised as I was.

"You must look different through the camera, Brian," said Sean Peters. "Watching you skate in real life, I didn't think you had The Look."

"You were the worst in the tryouts," said Madeline Chubb. "Even Sean was better. How come they picked you?"

"He only got the job because of his dad," sneered Kelvin Moray.

For once, Kelvin was right. Dad's company was paying for the ads, so he could give the part to his son if he wanted to. Dad thought being the Squeezee Kid would make me a legend at Garunga District School. Maybe he hoped it would take my mind off him and Mom splitting up. Dad didn't understand it would make me a total outcast.

When I phoned him, he denied getting me the

part, of course. "Brian, believe me, I didn't have anything to do with it. Rob Bridey's the expert on these things so I left it entirely up to him. He said you had exactly The Look he wanted."

What Look was that? I wondered.

"He said he can work around your skating, Brian," said Dad. "This job is mainly about acting."

Was that it? Maybe I did have brilliant acting potential. Maybe Rob Bridey could see me as the supercool Squeezee Kid. I was the Ice Man after all. When I decided not to show my feelings, nobody could see behind my mask to the shy, insecure Brian Hobble underneath. Once I was in my costume in front of the camera, I'd become a completely different, totally improved person.

"I think your friends will be really surprised and impressed," said Dad.

Amazingly, he was right. At least, it worked on the one person in the world I really needed to impress.

"It ought to be a very interesting experience for you, Brian," said Cassie Wyman. "I'd really like to know more about acting. You're lucky to get the opportunity to act in a professional film shoot."

"I'll tell you all about it," I promised. This was good! I'd get another chance to talk to her, about something she was interested in.

"Actually," said Nathan Lumsdyke, "Brian probably won't need to act at all. Stage actors may actually need to portray different characters, but film actors just play themselves, actually."

"Yeah," said Vince. "Like when Herbie Galanos was awesome in that film *Smash Grab*. Herbie was a kickboxing champion, not an actor. He was just good at bashing people."

So all I needed to do was just play myself and let the camera do the rest. When it came to shooting the ad, I was absolutely, certainly, positively sure I'd be great. Maybe.

osculation n. os-kew-lay-shun. Complicated word for kissing. See also "smooching," "making out," "sucking face," etc. (Note: kissing is scary, disgusting, exciting, nice, fun, or totally embarrassing, depending on who you're doing it with . . . so I've heard people say.)

SHOOTING the ad was an even worse disaster than the casting session.

When I arrived at school on the Saturday morning, the playground was full of trucks. Cables stretched off in every direction. A team of men were rigging massive spotlights and testing a trolley with a large film camera on it.

Clipboard Lisa met me at the gate. "Brian, darling. Straight off to wardrobe, if you don't mind." She pointed to a classroom labeled "Makeup."

Brian Hobble walked into the makeup room. Half an hour later the Squeezee Kid walked out. I had on these cool baggy jeans, new sneakers, and a loose leather jacket. The sides of my head were shaved and my hair was spiked up in the middle like Storm's from Z Squad. Only, my hair was bright blue.

How to Kiss

By B. Hobble
(as seen on T.V.)

① { Take your gum out of your mouth and put it somewhere safe

② Push out lips in a cool, sexy way }

③ SHUT EYES } even if you are kissing a really beautiful person, or if your friends are watching

④ KISS — trying not to burp or make slurping noise

⑤ Say "WOW"...

I'd never looked so cool in my entire life.

"Hey, guys," called director Rob Bridey to his camera crew. "Check out the Squeezee Kid!"

The cameraman whistled. I was ready. The filming went well, for the first three minutes.

Something I hadn't expected was that when they make a film, they don't have to start with the first thing that happens in Scene One, then shoot Scene Two, and so on. They can shoot bits of the film in any order, and then afterward the editor chooses the best takes and shuffles the scenes around so the story makes sense.

The first thing they shot in the Squeezee Kid commercial was Scene Three—where I do my evil warlord smile. (That's the one where I raise one eyebrow and curl the corner of my lip. If you want to learn to do it yourself, tape one eyebrow down with sticky tape and practice raising the other one in front of a mirror. When you do it right, you look really cool and totally inscrutable. After you take the sticky tape off, of course.)

Rob Bridey got me to sit on the ground, with my Rollerblades stuck out in front of me, suck on a Squeezee, then do The Smile to the camera. I only had to do it three times before he said, "Cut! Great work, kid."

Then it got a bit harder. When the gorgeous Tiffany came out of the makeup room.

And we had to do Scene Five . . . the kissing

scene. There hadn't been any kissing scene in the casting session. Maybe they were worried they'd get three million boys trying out for the part, just so they could kiss Tiffany.

First in Scene Five, I had to offer Tiffany the Squeezee. That was much easier to do without skating toward her the way I did in the casting session. I just had to sit next to her and hold out the drink box. Easy.

"Like a Squeezee?" I asked.

"Yes pleasee," sighed Tiffany. She put those perfect lips around the straw and sucked.

Rob Bridey called, "Great, Tiffany honey. Now look into Brian's eyes and give him a big kiss." This was it. In two seconds I was going to get a kiss from Tiffany!!! I'd never kissed any girl before, and now I was going to start on a girl that every right-minded boy in the entire world would want to kiss. Wait till I told my friends about it. Thank you, Dad, for getting me this part! This would change my life! Every boy would want to be me, and every girl would want to be next to kiss the coolest dude in Garunga!

Tiffany leaned over and gave me a nervous peck on the cheek. I'd had more passionate kisses from Mom's auntie Hilda.

"Cut!" called Rob Bridey. "Not like that, Tiffany! Hey, he's not your grandma, is he, darling? Give Brian a real big kiss on those luscious lips. Imagine you really love this cool guy who's just given you the greatest drink you've ever had in your life. Take two!"

We tried again.

"Like a Squeezee?" I said.

"Yes, pleasee," said Tiffany.

This time our noses banged together.

"Cut!" called Rob. "Take three."

One more try.

"Like a Squeezee?" I said.

"Yes, pleasee," said Tiffany.

This time she kissed me right on the mouth. I tried to kiss her back.

Tiffany was wearing really thick lip gloss. Her kiss tasted of that muck you smear on cold sores. It was like the time when our bathroom light blew. I couldn't find the toothpaste in the dark, and by mistake I brushed my teeth with Mom's shoe polish.

"Cut!" called Rob Bridey. "That was terrible! Like really, really lifeless and really, really bad! Can't you give it a bit of a zoom? I want to see you get right in there!"

Oh no! What was I doing wrong? I shouldn't have thought about the lip gloss. Maybe I ought to wiggle my cheeks around like film stars did. Or stick my tongue in her mouth.

Then I realized Rob wasn't talking to Tiffany and me. He was telling the crew to get the camera to zoom closer to us when we did the kiss. "Sorry, Brian and Tiffany, you were fine. You dudes relax while we set up the shot again."

Relax? Impossible, sitting next to Tiffany. While the crew swarmed around moving the lights and camera, we sat side by side in an awkward silence. I didn't know what to say to her. No way was I going to tell her that I'd just been kissed for the first time. Well, it was the first time if you didn't count that awful day, years ago in the elementary school sandbox, when Madeline Chubb asked me to marry her, and I said yes.

Amazingly, Tiffany broke the silence. What she said was even more amazing. "I'm sorry, Brian. I'm probably not very good at this. That's the first time I've kissed a boy."

You're kidding! This gorgeous girl who looked so super cool and confident was telling me that I was the first guy she'd ever kissed?

"Er, that's all right, er, Tiffany. Um, er (squeak, ahem . . .), I haven't kissed anyone before either." There, I'd said it!

"Honestly, Brian? I thought you must have, after all that acting you've done."

It was time for another confession. "Um, Tiffany, I'm not so great at acting. This is the first time I've been on TV."

"Really? Oh phew, that makes me feel so much better. I've never even acted in a school play. I just got this part because I could Rollerblade a bit. But Brian, you're a natural! You did that weird smiling scene so brilliantly."

Girls are funny. Just when you're trying to impress them with how great you are at something, you find out they like you even more when you say you're hopeless. I was just about to tell Tiffany about my Talking Rock experience, but the lights were ready and we went on to kissing scene, take four.

It took ten takes to get it right. After take five, some of Tiffany's lip gloss was wearing off. I even started to enjoy it a bit. By take eight I didn't feel I had to wipe my mouth after each kiss. After take ten, Rob Bridey called, "Wow, I'm happy! That was just a fantastic, awesome performance. Guys, you were hot that time!"

Again he was talking to the camera crew, not us.

"Did we do the kissing all right, Rob?" I asked.

He hardly seemed to notice me. "Sure, dude, fine. Cool." He went on explaining to the cameraman where to put the lights for the next scene.

Tiffany shook my hand rather stiffly, and said, "Thank you, Brian. I hope maybe we can work together again some time." Then she smiled shyly. "I'm glad it was you."

"Um, I'm glad it was me, too, Tiffany." It didn't feel like the coolest thing I could have said. Tiffany slipped her sunglasses back on and skated smoothly off toward the makeup room.

I still had another scene to shoot. My Roller-blading one.

premonition *n.* pre-mo-ni-shun.
Spine-tingling, gut-churning
feeling you get that you can see
into the future, where something is
about to go horribly wrong.

I teetered on top of the ramp.

Was it my imagination, or had they made it even higher than it had been at the casting session? My hands clung to the rail in a white-knuckled grip, like a zombie squeezing the life out of a baby kitten.

"Brian, dude," called Rob, "where's that smile we saw before, man? Chill out a bit."

Chill out? I was about to slip to my death off a squillion-foot-high ramp, with everybody in the world watching me on TV. I twisted the corner of my mouth and did my best to raise the eyebrow. Air hissed in and out of my nostrils in short, nervous breaths. I didn't feel the slightest bit like the cool Squeezee Kid. More like that little boy Eric on *Zombie Squad* when he's trapped in the dead-end alley with three huge zombies moving in to suck out his eyeballs. And there was no chance of Big Boy's rhino bursting through the wall to save me.

"Great!" called Rob. "That's perfect, Brian. Let's go for a take, guys!"

Really? Maybe I was a natural actor with The Look. Maybe I was fooling them all, and even though it felt shocking on the inside, my face looked really cool on the outside.

I took a quick suck on the asthma puffer to get rid of the small zombie who'd somehow sneaked into my chest and was crushing my windpipe. Then I did the smile. Rob was happy. "Classy work, Brian dude!" he called.

Bad places to land on ROLLERbLADES

Nº 3

School Principal's Desk

Skating between the Squeezee packs was next. Mr. Mackington has a sticker on his briefcase. It says "Everything that *can* go wrong, *will* go wrong." I never really understood it before, but now I knew exactly what it meant. It was about Rollerblading in front of a TV camera.

I was supposed to weave coolly and confidently between the packs and scoop up the last one to show to the camera.

Instead, I fell over. Over and over again. I fell on the ramp. I fell on the concrete. I fell on the Squeezee packs. Once I rolled out of control and crashed into the camera. My feet and legs had a mind of their own, and went off on expeditions wherever they liked. Madeline Chubb was absolutely, totally, 110 percent right. No way could I skate well enough to do a TV ad.

Finally, after take 27,974,846, Rob called, "Cut. That's got to be it. Thanks, Brian baby, we'll leave it there. Blades off, man. Go back to wardrobe and get changed. That's a wrap for you, dude."

I didn't get it. I hadn't done anything right, so they wouldn't be able to use the footage they'd shot.

"I'm sorry, Rob," I said.

"Brian, man, no problem. That was just what we needed. I'm happy, dude."

It was nice of him to try to cheer me up, but how could he be happy? Why was he letting me go before I'd managed to even weave between the Squeezee packs? Maybe my bad skating could be fixed with some special effects, which would make it look okay.

It wasn't until I was back in my own clothes and on my way to the school gate that I understood what was going on. Because out on the set they were filming another kid. He looked just like me—same jacket, same cool pants, and blue haircut like mine. Only this guy could skate. Really, really well.

I felt like Big Boy, the time Storm tells him he's screwed up once too often and he'll have to be replaced in Z Squad by another zombie fighter. My kissing had been too nervous and my skating had been hopeless. So I'd been dropped from the team. Someone else would have a chance to do the Rollerblading and the evil warlord smile and get to kiss Tiffany over and over.

And it was even harder for me than it had been for Big Boy. He hadn't been replaced by his worst enemy. The blue-headed Rollerblading kid taking over from me was Kelvin Moray.

Losing the part hurt. Each time I looked in the mirror at my blue hair, I felt a sharp pain, like Dr. Overcoat was stabbing me in the guts with a sharpened icicle. (He did that to Big Boy once, and then melted the icicle to destroy the murder weapon.) Because it turned out that the hair dye was permanent, and I'd have to wait for it to grow out.

When my friends asked me how the filming had gone, I acted my inscrutable Ice Man role, curling my lip into my evil warlord smile and saying, "You'll see." It would be a few days at least before the ad came on TV.

When Dad called to ask about the shoot, I just said, "It was okay."

"Rob Bridey was very pleased with you, Brian," said Dad. "He said you did a great job."

"Yeah, he told me that, too."

Dad must have known they'd replaced me. Of course he wouldn't want me to feel I'd let everybody down. He was just being encouraging.

Meanwhile, Kelvin Moray was very proud of his blue hair. He was telling everyone in the school how I turned out to be so hopeless at Rollerblading that he'd had to replace me as the Squeezee Kid. Strangely, he didn't say anything about kissing the gorgeous Tiffany. It certainly wouldn't be the first time Kelvin Moray had kissed a girl (he swapped girlfriends like other kids swapped football cards), so maybe he thought it was no big deal. Or maybe he was just waiting to do his boasting till everyone had seen him kissing Tiffany on TV.

I tried to shut it out of my mind. That suddenly became easier to do, because what happened next was much worse, and even freakier than me being replaced as the Squeezee Kid.

possession n. po-ze-shun. Something that someone owns, or something that completely takes a person over in a really freaky way, so it sends them totally out of control. (See also "crazy," "mad," "insane," "loopy," "psycho," etc.)

TO: Lancelot_Cummins@lancelotcummins.com
FROM: Brian.Hobble@supernet.com
SUBJECT: Urgent! Please stop Zombie Squad!

Dear Lance,
Please get *Zombie Squad* taken off TV right now!
  This is urgent and important!!!!!!!!!!
  Your fan,
  Brian Hobble
  P.S. This is not a joke!!!!!!

TO: Brian.Hobble@supernet.com
FROM: Lancelot_Cummins@lancelotcummins.com
SUBJECT: Re: Urgent! Please stop Zombie Squad!

Dear Brian,

I thought you liked *Zombie Squad*. What's the problem?

    Best wishes,

    Lancelot Cummins

TO: Lancelot_Cummins@lancelotcummins.com
FROM: Brian.Hobble@supernet.com
SUBJECT: This is serious!!!!!!!!

Dear Lance,

I know it sounds a bit weird. Don't get me wrong, I still like *Zombie Squad*.

    But it's really freaking out my little brother, Matthew. Please, please, please, stop it now!!!!!!!!!!!!!!!!

    Brian Hobble

TO: Brian.Hobble@supernet.com
FROM: Lancelot_Cummins@lancelotcummins.com
SUBJECT: Re: This is serious!!!!!!!!

Dear Brian,

Zombie Squad is not really meant for younger children, and I understand the program may possibly disturb them. They sometimes have trouble distinguishing fact from fantasy and believe that *Zombie Squad* is real.

    Maybe you should encourage Matthew to watch something else?

Best wishes,

Lancelot Cummins

P.S. You haven't sent me a story for a while. How's your writing going?

TO: Lancelot_Cummins@lancelotcummins.com
FROM: Brian.Hobble@supernet.com
SUBJECT: Sorry if this clogs up your e-mail system, but it's important!!!!

Dear Lance,

This is a bit of a long message, because I really need to tell you what's happening to Matthew, so you'll know why *Zombie Squad* has to be stopped.

This guy named Kelvin Moray invites Matthew around to his house every day after school, and they watch *Zombie Squad* together. Mom says he can go to Kelvin's because it's good for Matthew to mix with other boys and it takes a bit of pressure off me.

Mom doesn't understand that Kelvin is an idiot. She thinks I'm just jealous. Matthew likes to go there because he is young and stupid and thinks Kelvin is really cool.

But Lance, the really freaky thing with Matthew happened when I was teaching my little buddy, Sebastian, to play cricket . . .

Did I tell you this before, Lance? Sebastian thinks he's a fairy. I've persuaded him not to wear his fairy costume in public, so other kids won't bully him. I told Sebastian to be a disguised, plainclothes fairy, and he seems happy with that. His sister, Madeline, and I made him new wings, which he carries in his schoolbag, with his wand and flower garlands.

He still takes them everywhere he goes. Even when he came to my house for his first cricket lesson with Vince and me, he showed us that the pockets of his shorts were full of little bags of glittery stuff he calls fairy dust.

"Just in case I need to do a spell," he said.

"Fine, Sebastian," I said. "But keep that fairy dust out of sight when we're playing cricket. Do you like cricket? You know, it's like baseball."

"I love crickets!" said Sebastian.

"Really? That's great!"

"Pixies dance to the music of crickets," said Sebastian. "Grasshoppers, too."

"I mean cricket the game," I sighed. "I'm going to teach you to bowl and field and swing a bat."

Sebastian frowned. "Bats are dangerous."

"Not if you hold them carefully," I said.

"Bats bite you, Brian. And they fly around at night, with the bad goblins and evil boggarts riding them."

I took a deep breath and counted to ten. Teaching Sebastian to love cricket was harder than teaching a zombie to be kind to kittens.

"This is a cricket bat," I said firmly, pushing it into Sebastian's hands. "You're in."

"What am I in?" he asked.

"You're not in anything. You're just *in*. That's what they say in cricket, okay?"

"Oh," said Sebastian.

"You try to stay in and not get out."

"Get out of what, Brian?"

"Not out of anything. Just try not to get *out*, okay?"

"Oh. All right." Sebastian still sounded confused.

"Look, it's easy," I said. "When Vince bowls the ball to you, hit it with the bat."

Vince was bouncing a tennis ball impatiently at the end of our driveway.

"Why?"

"Sebastian, trust me. Just whack it as hard as you can."

I showed him how to stand, bat raised to waist height. "Just bowl, Vince," I called.

How to avoid being Bullied
No. 3

"Hide really well"

Vince lobbed a slow loopy ball in Sebastian's direction.

"Now hit, Sebastian!"

Sebastian gave a clumsy swipe, clunking the bat into my knee.

"Ow!" I said.

"Sorry," said Sebastian.

"It's all right," I gasped. "Only next time try to hit the ball."

Vince prepared to bowl again, but Sebastian put his bat down on the ground. "Just a minute, Brian." He poked his fingers into his pocket and pulled out a pinch of sparkly silver powder. "Time to use my fairy dust."

"I told you, Sebastian. No fairy dust when you're playing cricket."

"All right." Sebastian put the dust back in his pocket and wiped it off his fingers. "I'll just say a fairy spell." He thought for a moment, then waved his hands over the bat and chanted:

"Fairy magic, on this bat,

Make it hit the cricket ball, Whack! *Like that.*"

He mimed a big swing with the bat.

Maybe Sebastian had discovered the secret of the great cricketers of history. Lots of players had superstitions like never changing their socks when they were batting. Maybe the champions worked fairy spells on their bats before big games. Somehow I didn't think so.

Sebastian picked up the bat and faced down the pitch, a big smile on his face.

Vince bowled again. Sebastian took another swing. *Whack!* You wouldn't believe that a five-year-old could hit a ball so hard, especially not a five-year-old who sometimes wore cellophane wings. A zombie who'd drunk a whole flagon of reanimation fluid couldn't hit like that. The ball sailed over Vince's head, over the fence, over the road, and rolled away.

"Wow!" said Vince.

"Sorry," said Sebastian.

"No," I said, "that's what you're supposed to do. That was a great hit, Sebastian."

The ball trickled across the road and ended up in the gutter. An old homeless man, pushing a shopping cart along the street, stopped to pick it up.

(And Lance, I hope you're still reading this, because this is when things become really freaky . . .)

The old guy had just taken hold of the ball when I heard the *Zombie Squad* music. "Dee-da-dum dee daa, Z Squad, dumm-ditty-daa-daa, Zombie Squad ..." Now that I think about it, the music could have been coming from a passing car. Only I can't remember any cars passing at that moment. What I do remember is a zombie fighter zooming around the corner. It was Matthew, wearing his Z Squad belt and headband, but now with a silver cape flying out behind him.

Matthew was riding an imaginary eagle, like

Storm's special steed. He raced across the road, arms outstretched, and was swooping toward our front gate when the old man called out to him, "Whoa, easy does it, young feller-me-lad. Little chaps like you shouldn't run into the road, you know."

He tossed the tennis ball back to Matthew. Instead of catching it, Matthew shrank back against the fence, staring at the ball like it was a live hand grenade. The ball rolled back across the street toward the old man.

Matthew scurried inside the gate.

"What's wrong, Matthew?" I asked.

The blood drained from his face, like it did from Lisa's in your book *Nose Job*, remember, Lance? You know, on page sixty-one, where Professor Mucus has her trapped in his cellar and is about to gag her with a snot-filled handkerchief.

"Look at his torn jacket!" gasped Matthew, pointing at the old man, who was now moving toward him, holding out the ball. I saw now that the lining of the man's coat had torn and was hanging loose. Matthew spoke into his wristwatch. "Zombie sighting! Zombie sighting! Mitzi, Big Boy, are you receiving me? This is Storm. Come in, Z Squad!"

The old man had reached the gate now and leaned over to give the ball to Matthew. Matthew snarled at him, in a perfect imitation of Storm's voice, "You don't scare me with that zombie hand grenade. Z Squad to the rescue!"

The music seemed to get louder. Matthew rushed at the old man and threw a flying karate kick at him. His foot slammed into the man's arm, knocking the ball from his hand and sending him spinning back from the gate.

"Hey, steady on, young feller!" called the old man. "I'm only trying to help you."

Matthew swung into a kung fu pose and launched his fist up at the old man's head. The old man reeled back and just avoided it. I ran to grab Matthew around the waist. Matthew kicked and struggled like he was having some sort of fit. The old man hobbled off down the street, clutching his forearm and pushing his cart with his good hand. Matthew screamed at him, "Never give up, never give in! You zombies will never defeat the power of Zirgon!"

Vince pinned Matthew's arms. We wrestled him to the ground, but even with our combined weight, we could hardly hold him down.

"What's the matter with him, Brian?" yelled Vince.

"Matthew's obsessed with *Zombie Squad*. He thinks it's real."

"Let me up!" screamed Matthew. "You're letting the zombie get away!"

"You're crazy," I yelled into his ear. "That's just a harmless old guy who brought our ball back."

Matthew screamed, and I was tossed into the air. It felt like the time a volcano erupted under Big Boy. I crashed heavily on the driveway and shut my eyes.

Suddenly a little voice chanted . . .

*"Fairy magic, sugar and spice,
No more fighting! All be nice!"*

When I blinked my eyes open, Matthew was lying in a limp heap on the ground. He was quiet for a moment. I saw the blood return to his face, like it did to Lisa's face in *Nose Job* when she realized Dr. Mucus wasn't going to stick the snotty hanky in her mouth, but just wanted to blow his nose. Then Matthew stood up, rubbing his eyes. "Brian, can I bat next?"

He didn't know that anything unusual had happened! Sebastian tucked a bag of fairy dust back into his pocket and smiled at me. "I didn't use the fairy dust, Brian, so the bullies didn't see it," he whispered.

Lance, this is getting really freaky. I don't believe in fairies, any more than I believe in zombies, but Sebastian seemed to have done something magic to Matthew. And it was lucky that he did, because if Sebastian is weird, Matthew is even worse. *Zombie Squad* is making Matthew totally mad, crazy, deranged, loco, unhinged, and loopy. If his brain was a soccer team it would be playing a man short.

Lance, that's why you have to please stop *Zombie Squad*. It's dangerous!!!!!!!!!!

Please help!

Brian Hobble

Dear Brian,

Well done in writing such a gripping story. I love your funny version of the cricket lesson, and it's exciting to see how you've developed Matthew into a crazy Z Squad fan. I hope he doesn't attack old men in the street in real life! Sebastian is quite a charming little character, too. Did you base him on anybody you know?

Z Squad's Guide to Zombie fighting techniques   Nº 4

"The VERTICAL Slice"

Seriously, Brian, do you really think *Zombie Squad* is too violent? Or were you just inventing that to make your story more dramatic?

Incidentally, although I wrote the original *Z Squad* books, I have no control over the TV series. I sold my rights to the television production company, and while I'm entitled to be consulted on the storylines, I can only offer my opinion, and in the end the contract allows the producers to do whatever they like. I certainly wouldn't be able to have *Zombie Squad* removed from the TV screens now. That's up to the network and the sponsors whose advertising pays for the show.

Between you and me, I'm not happy with the way the stories have become more violent than they were in the books. I much prefer to have my heroes solve problems by using their wits to defeat the bad guys, but the martial arts fight scenes are popular with viewers, according to the market research. Apparently kids love heroes bashing up monsters!

I'll pass on your concern to the producers, but since the programs have now been recorded, I'm afraid it's unlikely they'd want to make changes. Well, that's the end of my lecture on the hard, cruel world of commercial TV. It's been a learning experience for me, too!

Best wishes, and keep on with your own writing, Brian. You're doing very well!

Lance

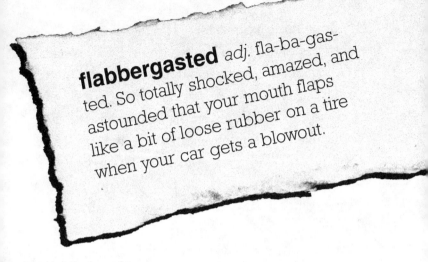

flabbergasted adj. fla-ba-gas-ted. So totally shocked, amazed, and astounded that your mouth flaps like a bit of loose rubber on a tire when your car gets a blowout.

THE only good thing about the freaky stuff with Matthew and Sebastian was it had stopped me thinking about the Great Squeezee Kid Disaster.

So what happened next took me completely by surprise.

I was arriving at school when a little kid called out, "Like a Squeezee?" He giggled and ran away.

Abby and Sofie and Sarah, who have bubblegum for brains, were next. As I walked into the English classroom they were waiting for me. They chanted, "Like a Squeezee?" and then, "Yes pleasee!" Then they made kissing noises and dissolved into helpless giggles, like Mitzi when Dr. Overcoat strapped her on the Laughter Machine, where zombies tickle people to death.

All day, kids were nudging each other and giggling in my direction. Everywhere I went, I heard a chorus of "Like a Squeezee?" It rang in my ears like one of those songs you can't get out of your head.

"What's all this Squeezee stuff about, Brian?" asked Cassie Wyman. So there was one other person apart from me who didn't know the answer to that one. Cassie liked reading more than watching TV. She was the only kid in our class who'd never seen *Zombie Squad*.

Even Vince and Sean wouldn't tell me what it was all about.

"You mean, you haven't seen it?" snorted Vince. "Man, you're famous!"

"Brian, you're a star!" said Sean. "Have a look at *Zombie Squad* tonight."

Everyone seemed to think I was famous, but how could I be? Why wasn't Kelvin Moray the famous one?

Matthew went home with Kelvin after school, so I was home on my own. I switched on *Zombie Squad*.

Frogmen zombies were driving a pod of whales into shallow water so that they would beach themselves and die. I was totally shocked, appalled, disgusted, horrified, and flabbergasted. Not by the zombies, but by what came on in the first ad break. It was the Squeezee commercial, and it went like this:

Scene 1: Tiffany Rollerblades brilliantly, weaving between the Squeezee packs, looking totally and utterly to die for.

Scene 2: The Squeezee Kid (played by B. Hobble) watches her from the top of the ramp. He has The Look of a Complete Idiot. The blue hair and groovy costume looked totally stupid on me. My evil warlord smile was a pathetic attempt to look cool. You could see the fear in my eyes as I clung to the rail on top of the ramp. Worst of all was the voiceover, announcing, "This is The Kid Who Sucks."

Scene 3: The Squeezee Kid lets go of the rail and skates down the ramp. He falls over. He falls over again. He falls over once more. He sits hard on his butt on a Squeezee pack. He falls again . . .

They'd used take after take of my most embarrassing moments, all cut quickly together. The Kid Who Sucks was obviously the worst Rollerblader since the Big Bang.

Scene 4: The Kid Who Sucks (you guessed it, me again) sitting on the ground, blades stuck out at a ridiculous angle, sucks a Squeezee and gives a try-hard evil warlord smile. The announcer's voice reminds anyone who's forgotten, "The Kid *really* sucks."

Scene 5: The Squeezee Kid jumps to his feet and skates brilliantly between the packs on the ground. That Squeezee drink has magically made him a great blader. How did they do that? I'd never skated like that. It was only when I saw it again in the second ad break that I realized we can only see the Rollerblader from the back. This was my stunt double, Kelvin Moray.

Scene 6: The Squeezee Kid meets the lovely Tiffany and asks, "Like a Squeezee?" "Yes pleasee!" she replies and . . . horror of horrors . . . there was that kiss!

They'd used take ten. It was the best kiss we'd done but, as our lips met, there was the appalling announcer's voice, triumphantly announcing, "The Kid Who Sucks—sucks good!" And as the Squeezee logo came up on the screen, I smiled at the camera, not my twisted evil warlord smile this time, but the totally happy, totally unfaked, totally relieved smile I'd given when Rob Bridey had said "cut" and we didn't need to do any more kissing.

That was it. Life as I'd known it up till now was over. Until the day I died, I'd be known at Garunga District School, and probably throughout the entire country, not as supercool Brian (The Ice Man) Hobble. Now I was "The Kid Who Sucks."

I understood why child film star Chadley Stevens had stolen that packet of bubblegum. If he was locked up in jail, he wouldn't have to face his friends at school.

repercussions *n.* ree-per-ku-
shuns. When things that you've
done cause waves that come
back and hit you on the head like
the drums and cymbals in a very
loud band.

"BRIAN, we can't take the ad off TV and that's
that."

"I'm a total laughingstock, Dad!"

"No you're not, son," said Dad. "People really like
it. It's funny and memorable and viewers love it. My
boss is over the moon. He called me in to his office
and congratulated me personally. Squeezee sales are
going through the roof."

"Dad, everywhere I go, people whisper 'Kid Who
Sucks' and 'Like a Squeezee?'"

"That will pass, Brian. When that blue fades out
of your hair they won't even recognize you. Kids
wouldn't be buying Squeezee drinks if they didn't
think they were cool. Young people all over the
country want to be like The Kid Who Sucks. In fact,
my boss is suggesting you do another Squeezee Kid
ad, this time about surfing."

"I can't surf, Dad. I'll fall off the board. I'll sink. I'll drown. What if I get eaten by a shark?"

"Brian, this means a lot to me, son, and it's going really well. Just think about it, that's all I ask. Please."

"Anything you say, Dad."

The fact that I was the Squeezee Kid explained one thing. I now knew why Kelvin Moray never mentioned kissing Tiffany. He didn't want everyone to hear that he didn't have The Look, so he only got to stand in for me in the skating scenes. He never kissed Tiffany at all. I was pleased about that. I didn't like the idea of my first-kiss girl getting her face sucked ten minutes later by my worst enemy.

While Kelvin zoomed around the school showing off his skating tricks, the only question everybody asked me was, "What was it like kissing that girl?"

"Did you really kiss her yourself, Brian?" asked Sean.

"'Course he did," said Vince. "We saw him."

"It could have been a trick of the camera," said Sean. "Maybe he had a stand-in. You know, someone who's a real top professional kisser."

"I did all my own kissing stunts," I said.

"And? What was it like?" asked Vince.

Now The Kid Who Sucks could really impress his friends. I shrugged modestly. "Not bad," I said. "Though if I don't say so myself, it wasn't too bad for her either. She even deliberately screwed up a take so she could kiss me again . . ."

Then I saw Cassie Wyman standing behind Vince and Sean, eyes boring into me like a zombie deciding whether to eat my brains or my liver first. Kissing Cassie Wyman would be even scarier than kissing Tiffany, because I really liked Cassie. Maybe Cassie liked me, too, but she'd never kissed me. And if she heard me boasting about kissing Tiffany, she never would.

"Come on, Brian," said Vince, "tell us more gory details!"

I was trapped, like Big Boy when he has to choose between saving Eric or Mitzi from the zombies. I couldn't use my evil warlord smile to avoid the question. I'd seen that smile on TV, and I knew how stupid it looked. It needed a lot more practice in front of the bathroom mirror before I could use it again in public.

I said, "Er . . . um . . . really, the whole kissing thing, it's just acting. The trick is to make it look like you're crazy about the girl, even if you don't like her."

Cassie Wyman hooked me up to that Truth Machine. Only it wasn't just her asking the questions. Sean and Vince were in on the act, too.

"But *did* you like her? What was her name, Brian?" asked Cassie.

"Tiffany . . . um." (*Truth Machine flat.*)

"Tiffany!" sighed Vince. "Was she as hot as she looked, Brian?"

"All right, I suppose." (*Truth Machine blips quietly.*

Tiffany was hot but I can't say so in front of Cassie.)

"Was she a good kisser?" asked Sean.

Boy, this was a tricky one. I'd never been kissed by anyone else, so I didn't know what good kissing was supposed to be like. No way could I tell my friends how awkward it had been kissing Tiffany. I'd hinted to them that the kissing was great and that I was fantastic at it. But I couldn't let Cassie see me boasting to my friends.

My brain searched frantically through the rubble in its back shed, and just in time came across the perfect answer for my mouth to spout out. Cassie was watching my face carefully, monitoring the Truth Machine's reaction.

I said, "Tiffany was completely professional. It was a pleasure to act with someone who knows their craft." (*Truth Machine bleeps uncertainly. It doesn't know what that answer meant either. Little prickles run down my arms, but no major shocks.*) Phew! Brian Hobble, you are a genius! In two sentences I'd switched the whole interrogation from the art of kissing to the art of acting.

"Were you nervous acting in front of the camera?" asked Cassie.

"At first I was, but you get used to all the people watching." (*Yowch! Truth Machine gives me a major electric shock. I'd been totally terrified from start to finish.*)

"Was the director nice?" asked Cassie. "Did he teach you a lot about acting?"

43

Rob Bridey hadn't taught me anything about acting. He'd deliberately made me scared and then just filmed me trying to look cool. I couldn't tell Cassie that Rob Bridey had totally used me.

I said, "Rob was great. He explained before we filmed it that The Kid Who Sucks has to look really nervous to start with, and skate really badly. Then when he's had a Squeezee he has to completely change into someone super cool and confident. It's quite a demanding acting task." (*Bzzzzt! Aarrghhh! That Truth Machine is killing me. Dr. Overcoat cackles an evil laugh. He knows what a liar I am.*)

"Are they making more Squeezee Kid ads, Brian?" asked Cassie.

"Er, maybe." (*True answer. Not even a blip from the Truth Machine.*)

"Cool! Will you get to kiss Tiffany again?" asked Vince.

"Um . . ."

"Will you?" asked Cassie.

". . . sure, I mean yes, I mean . . ." (*Bzzzzzzzzzzzttttttt! Aaaaaaaaaaaarrrgghhhh!!!!!!!!*)

I was relieved when Nathan Lumsdyke dragged Cassie away. "I actually finished my picture book, if you'd like to read it, Cass. It's actually quite educational, about the history of Garunga . . ."

Phew!

paranoia *n.* pa-ra-noy-a.
Being scared stiff because
people you see around you
look like flesh-eating zombies.

MATTHEW seemed a bit calmer when his fairy companion, Sebastian, was around. He still talked about Z Squad constantly, but he'd stopped acting it out. For the next day or two he preferred coming home with me to going to Kelvin's, as long as Sebastian came, too, and we played backyard cricket. Sebastian had learned to bowl straight and even hit the ball occasionally without the aid of fairy spells. Things were going better. Until the day we met the bikers.

Matthew and Sebastian were walking home with me. Sebastian always held my hand, although I stopped him doing it until we were away from the school, so none of my friends would see. Today, as we crossed Branxton Park, Matthew grabbed my hand, too, and clutched it in a death grip.

"Ouch! What's wrong with you, Matthew?" I said.

"It's dangerous here," hissed Matthew.

"It's the middle of the afternoon, in a nice quiet neighborhood. What are you worried about?"

45

"Zombies," whispered Matthew.

"For the last time," I said, "*Zombie Squad* isn't real!"

Matthew's eyes darted from side to side as we made our way through the clump of trees by the swings in the children's adventure playground. A mother held a giggling toddler on the little slide. A man was feeding bread to ducks on the lake.

"Zombies in disguise!" whispered Matthew.

"They're not zombies, Matthew. They don't even have torn clothes."

"They might be clever zombies, with sewing machines," said Matthew. "Maybe they fixed the rips in their coats."

"Listen, Matthew, you can't spend your life worrying about people who want to scare you." I remembered the speech Storm made to wimpy little Eric. "You just have to tell yourself that no matter what they do, or how scary they seem, they can't stop good ordinary people getting on with their lives."

Matthew stared into my eyes and nodded. "I won't worry anymore, Brian. If zombies come here to Garunga, Z Squad will come to save us."

"And put a magic fairy spell on the zombies," said Sebastian.

"And kickbox them," said Matthew.

"Whatever," I said.

We walked on to the crossing at Greville Street. Two huge motorcycles were parked there. Parked on a bench were two huge bikers, wearing leather vests labeled across the back "Meat Man" and "Slasher." Meat Man seemed to have somehow stolen Slasher's hair. Meat Man's hair spread in a huge Afro, and he still had enough left over to make a curly ponytail down his back. Slasher was completely bald. The bikers' leather vests were old. With tears all over them.

Slasher turned casually to glance in our direction. Matthew instantly wheeled away from him and cupped his hands around the side of his head. "Don't let them look into your eyes, Brian! Run!"

But before we could take a step, Slasher nudged Meat Man and pointed at me. "Hey, Meat Man, we're having a brush with fame. That's The Kid Who Sucks!"

I saw now that both bikers were holding

The cape helps

The dopey ones are too slow to move

Steel-caps

Z Squad's Guide to ZOMBIE fighting TECHNIQUES Nº 5

By B. Hobble

Squeezees. Meat Man said, "Hey, Kid Who Sucks, where are your Rollerblades?"

Slasher took Meat Man's Squeezee and walked over to us. "Go on, Kid, do that skating trick for me." He placed the Squeezees on the footpath and stepped back.

Matthew dashed forward. He dived at the Squeezees, rolled on the grass like a Z Squad hero avoiding a laser beam, and came up holding a packet in each hand.

"Hey!" said Slasher.

He grabbed at Matthew, but Matthew was quicker. He pointed the Squeezees at Slasher, and yelled, "By the power of Zirgon, I command you to liquefy!"

Then he crushed the Squeezees. Two streams of yellow liquid squirted straight into the bikers' faces.

"Matthew! What are you doing?" I yelled.

"Zombies hate water, Brian," screamed Matthew. "When Z Squad wet them, they shrink."

Meat Man and Slasher didn't shrink. Once they'd wiped the juice out of their eyes with the backs of their hairy hands, they seemed to grow about nine feet taller (or, in Meat Man's case, wider).

"I'll get you, you little weed!" growled Slasher.

Meat Man added a few thoughts of his own, including some words I'd never heard before, but I didn't think it was the best time to ask him what they meant.

"Run!" I yelled.

We ran. We had the advantage of surprise and a short start. And we were scared. Having bikers chasing you makes you really fast. If we were riding a cheetah we couldn't have gotten around the corner into Branxton Park any quicker. As I glanced back I saw Meat Man and Slasher running down the street behind us. And catching up.

We had to hide. My eye caught sight of a loose picket in the high wooden fence that separated the park from the Garunga Shopping Mall beside it. The mall was a real maze. If we could get in there, the bikers would never find us, and if they did there'd be other people there to save us.

I pulled the fence picket aside. "Quick! Through here!" I yelled.

Matthew dived through it first, then I bundled Sebastian into it. The little boys ran off toward the safety of the mall. I was bigger than them. And bigger than the gap in the fence. But having bikers chasing you makes you more supple, like when Storm drank bone-dissolving potion and turned into a jellyfish. Somehow I oozed my body through the gap in the fence. My jellyfish arms had just enough strength to push the fencing back into place.

I was just turning to run after Matthew and Sebastian when the fence seemed to explode open. A giant hairy paw swept the loose board aside. Meat Man's head appeared in the gap. His neck followed . . . and his shoulders. The gap was far too small for him, but his hands were ripping the fence apart and he'd soon have a hole wide enough for Big Boy and his rhinoceros to fit through.

Then Slasher climbed over the top of the fence above Meat Man. I'd been wishing the fence had been stronger, but suddenly I was glad it wasn't. It collapsed under Slasher's weight. He came down on top of Meat Man, the two of them tangled in a mess of splintered wood and a whole jumble of colorful language, including lots of new and interesting words and expressions, which any writer would find very useful. Only I couldn't hang around to note them for future use.

"Run, Brian!" called Matthew.

My left leg ran. My right leg felt like it was caught in one of those metal shackles Dr. Overcoat uses to chain up victims in his underground dungeon, before he feeds them to his zombies for breakfast. I was caught, trapped, incarcerated, manacled, and frozen to the spot. Meat Man's hand was clamped around my ankle. Slasher took hold of my arm.

They held a brief meeting at which they decided what to do with me. I can't list the exact words they used or Ms. Kitto would ban this book from the school library. I can only say the plans they had for me were not pleasant.

But before they could carry out their dastardly threats, Sebastian's little voice piped up:

> "Fairy magic,
> Sugar and spice,
> Make bad zombies
> Turn out nice!"

He was wearing his wings and flower garland. He was waving his wand.

The effect was remarkable, extraordinary, amazing, unpredictable, and totally not what anyone would have expected. You would think that bikers like Slasher and Meat Man would smash fairies into little pieces. Instead, they smiled.

Meat Man let go of my ankle and reached over to straighten the garland of flowers, which was slipping down over Sebastian's eyes.

"Isn't he cute?" said Meat Man.

"The sweetest little guy I ever saw!" agreed Slasher.

I couldn't believe this! I felt the wheezing start in my chest. There seemed to be a bit of an interval in the drama, so I had time to take out my asthma inhaler and give my lungs a quick boost.

From the corner of the flats, Matthew called, "Kickbox them, Brian! Smash them to pieces! Go on, Brian, bash the zombies up! Kill them!"

Slasher gave Matthew a friendly wave. "Hi there, little fellow."

I took Sebastian's hand and carefully led him over to Matthew. I took Matthew's hand, too. My heart was pounding, but the rest of me was in Ice Man mode. I made the little boys walk very quietly till we were out of sight of Slasher and Meat Man.

Then we ran into the mall. At least, Sebastian and I ran into the mall. Matthew stood transfixed, staring at a billboard just outside the entrance.

There was a picture of Storm, Big Boy, and Mitzi fighting zombies. The words across their stomachs said:

power of persuasion n.
powr-ov-pur-sway-shun. Making someone change their mind by using a sensible well-reasoned argument, promising them a chocolate cookie, or threatening to bash them.

MY little brother was completely crazy. He had a major rattle in his upstairs gearbox. But he was still my little brother. If he saw Z Squad live and in person, right here in Garunga, he'd never believe they weren't real. I had to stop him from seeing the show.

Mom was already worried enough about the inside of my head. She'd never believe my story about Matthew attacking a biker gang with loaded Squeezees. A freaky story like that would make her think it was me who was going crazy. Instead, I tried to have a grown-up, man-to-man talk with Dad.

"Sun River Fruits is sponsoring this show. You could have it stopped if you wanted to."

"Ye-es we could, Brian." Dad scratched his chin.

"But why should we? *Zombie Squad* is the top-rated kids' program on TV at the moment. Thanks to Z Squad and your Squeezee Kid ad, we're getting great publicity."

"Dad, your company wants to be associated with doing good things for young people. Squeezees shouldn't be encouraging kids to flatten people with flying dropkicks."

"I think you're exaggerating a bit, Brian. Everyone knows *Zombie Squad* is a complete fantasy." Not quite everyone knows that, I thought. "Our special events department says *Z Squad Live* is harmless musical entertainment for the whole family. Kids love it."

"You haven't seen it, Dad."

"I will. I'm taking Matthew along on Saturday."

I reached across the table and took Dad by both shoulders. Then I lowered my voice, raised both eyebrows, and stared deep into Dad's eyes without blinking, the way Storm does when he wants to use the Power of Persuasion.

"Dad, this is very important. It is urgent and vital that you do not take Matthew to see this show."

Dad cocked his head to one side. "Brian, are you all right? Your eyes look funny."

I dropped my voice to an intense whisper, the way Storm did when he knew zombies were going to attack the school sports carnival and he had to warn little Eric not to go in the sack race. "Please, Dad, trust me on this one."

Dad looked a little shocked. He laid a hand on one of mine and his voice trembled slightly as he muttered, "All right, Brian. Er, you know your mother and I both love you. We'd do anything to make you happy. I'll go and check out the show myself."

"Without Matthew?"

"Without Matthew."

Persuading Mom was easier.

"I'll stay home and look after Matthew while you go shopping, Mom. You'll find it much easier to get around Garunga Mall if you don't have Matthew hanging on to your ankles."

"Thank you, dear. Sure you two will be all right on your own?"

"Vince is coming over. We're finishing our Bessemer Converter science project. Mom, believe me, Matthew will stay here with us. He won't leave the house. I swear."

babysit *v.* bay-bee-sit. Look after a person when their parents aren't home. (Note: the person doesn't have to be a baby, although they sometimes behave like one.)

THUMP! *Thump! Thump!*
Thump! Thump! Thump!

The sound of a five-year-old hitting the back of a bedroom door gets really annoying after about three-and-a-half seconds. When it goes on for half an hour, it can totally drive you nuts.

"Let me out, Briiiiiiannnnn!" whined Matthew's voice.

"Shut up, Matthew."

Thump! Thump! Thump!
Thump! Thump! Thump!

"Let me out, Briiiiiannnn!"

"No way."

"Want to see Z *Squad Live!* Want to see Z *Squad Live!*"

"You can't see Z *Squad Live*, Matthew. Mom said you had to stay in your room till she gets home."

Thump! Thump! Thump!

Thump! Thump! Thump!

"It's no good, Matthew. You are not going to see Z *Squad Live* and that's that."

"Briiiiaaaannnnn!"

Vince glanced up at the clock on the living room wall. Nine twenty-one. Still an hour and thirty-nine minutes till the Z *Squad Live* show. Say it goes for about half an hour, that means it would still be two hours and nine minutes before the show was over.

"Can't we at least let him out, Brian?" asked Vince. "I'll give him a turn playing DeathTrap."

Ding-dong! The doorbell chimed cheerily. It was the only cheery thing I'd heard all morning. When I opened the door, I stopped feeling cheery. Kelvin Moray was on the doorstep, balancing on his Rollerblades. Behind him were Arthur Neerlander and Rocco Ferris.

"What do you want, Kelvin?"

"Is Matty home?"

"No."

Thump, thump, thump—from the bedroom door.

Kelvin called past me into the house, "Want to come to Z *Squad Live*, Matty?"

"No, he doesn't," I said. "He hates Z Squad."

"Since when?"

"Since his obsession with Z Squad nearly got us killed by zombie bikers," I said. "He thinks Z Squad is really stupid now and no way does he want to see them."

The whine came from behind the bedroom door again. "Want to see Z Squad! Want to see Z Squad!"

Kelvin Moray raised one eyebrow. I hate to admit it, but he did it pretty well. He looked exactly like an evil warlord.

"He's not allowed to go, Kelvin," I said. "You should never have encouraged Matthew's interest in a show totally unsuitable for someone of his age, and he's finding it very disturbing. Now if you don't mind, I'll have to ask you to leave quietly. It's Saturday morning and the neighbors may be sleeping in."

"It's a pity Matty's got an old woman like you for a brother, Brian," said Kelvin. He glanced over his shoulder at Arthur and Rocco. "No wonder the kid never has any fun."

I shut the door in his face. I thought I had shut it gently, but at that precise moment a huge crash resounded through the house. Matthew's bedroom door lay flat, its hinges clinging to chips of splintered wood. A small, localized tornado seemed to blast across the living room, knocking me sideways onto the sofa and ripping its way through the front door.

"Matthew!" I yelled. Vince and I rushed to the door. Kelvin Moray, Arthur, and Rocco were skating away down the driveway. Matthew was perched on Kelvin's shoulders.

It's funny how when you're desperate you can do things you're normally hopeless at. Only a few days ago I couldn't Rollerblade at all. Now Vince and I broke a world record as we skated down the street to Garunga Mall.

I was so busy being worried about Matthew that I didn't have time to worry about whether I was going to break my neck. My hand was tucked behind my back, and my free arm swung smoothly back and forward like Madeline Chubb's did. I was as cool as The Kid Who Sucks after he'd drunk his Squeezee.

We reached Garunga Mall in three minutes and sixteen seconds. The place was packed with moms and dads being towed along by little *Zombie Squad* fans. Everywhere you looked there were miniature clones of Storm or Mitzi. But no sign of Kelvin and Matthew.

"They know we're looking for them, Vince," I said. "They'll be hiding out until the show starts."

"I'll go around from the right," said Vince. "You start at the left."

"Right."

"No, you go left, Brian."

"I meant 'right, I'll go left,'" I said.

"Whatever," said Vince.

We split up. I searched shop after shop with no success. Woolfields, Pete's Meats, Hot Drop Cafe, Pampered Pooch Pet Salon . . . Kelvin and Matthew had vanished, as if they were wearing Z Squad invisibility belts.

Then I thought of the restrooms. I went into the

men's room. And stopped. There was a zombie in there, looking at himself in the mirror.

THE zombie was tall and thin. His woolen gloves had the fingers cut off and his nails were painted black. There was no need for me to check for rips in his clothes. I knew he was a zombie from his face. It was a deathly white, with dark rings around red-rimmed eyes.

My feet were rooted to the spot, like Mitzi's were the time Dr. Overcoat set them in concrete as he got ready to throw her into shark-infested waters. My mind searched feverishly for a plan.

It came up with three of them:

Plan A: Kickbox zombie, splash him with water, and shrink him.

Plan B: Don't attempt to do any kickboxing, just back calmly and quietly out of door and notify police, mall manager, and Z Squad.

Plan C: Run away screaming my head off.

I didn't have time to do any of my plans. "Hey,"

growled the zombie, waggling a bony finger at me, "I-know-you!"

"I . . . d-don't think so," I stammered.

"Oh-yes-I-do. I-haff-seen-you." I tried to lift my feet out of the concrete as the zombie came toward me. I couldn't. He gripped my shoulder and peered into my face, a bit like Madeline Chubb does, only without the smell of Nutter Butters. "I-know-I-haff-seen-you!"

A toilet flushed in one of the stalls. The zombie whipped around as the door opened, and Storm from Z Squad appeared, hitching up the shoulder straps on his tight red zombie-fighting suit.

This was totally freaky. Just when I was going to have my eyeballs sucked out, Z Squad had come to save me! But what Storm said was nothing like the dialogue they had on the TV show. "How come they don't put zippers on these suits?" he asked the zombie.

"You are a sup-er her-o, Storm," chanted the zombie. "Sup-er her-oes nev-er have to pee." He spun me around to face Storm and suddenly spoke like a normal person. "Who's this guy, Geoff? Where have I seen him before?"

Storm stared at me, too. Then the zombie snapped his fingers and said, "Got it! This is the Squeezee Kid."

"The Kid Who Sucks!" grinned Storm. "I love that ad! Man, you gave a great performance! Let me shake your hand."

The penny was starting to drop. This zombie was not a real zombie. This Storm was not a real zombie fighter. These were the actors from *Z Squad Live*.

The zombie said, "Who are you really, Kid Who Sucks?"

"Brian Hobble."

"Brian Hobble," said Storm. "Remember that name, folks. When he wins an Academy Award for Best Actor in a Major Motion Picture, we'll be able to say we once met him in Garunga Mall."

"You liked the Squeezee ad?" I asked.

The zombie turned back to the mirror and added stitches to his scar with a thin black makeup stick. "Man, all ads suck. They're just the consumer society telling us money can buy us happiness. But, Brian Hobble, I love your performance up on that ramp. You can tell the Squeezee Kid's terrified on those skates, but he's trying not to show it in front of the girl. Brilliant acting!"

It was nice to have my acting admired, even if it was a zombie doing the admiring. Should I tell him that I hadn't really been acting, and I only looked totally terrified in the ad because I *was* totally terrified?

"That weird twisted smile," said Storm. "Could you show me how to do that?"

"I don't know . . . ," I said.

"Hey, go on, Brian man, nobody's gonna see it except us," said the zombie.

I raised my eyebrow and curled the corner of my lip in my best evil warlord impression. Storm and the zombie roared with laughter.

"Fantastic, Brian!" howled Storm. "That's the funniest thing I've ever seen."

"Z Squad fan, are you, Brian?" asked the zombie. "Did you come to the mall specially to see our sophisticated artistic show today?"

"My little brother Matthew's into *Zombie Squad*," I said. "I'm a bit over it now."

"That's what the big cool dudes always say," Storm smiled. "Between you and me and the walls, we're pretty over it, too, aren't we, Ian?" The zombie's real name was Ian? Well, even zombies have to be called something.

Storm squatted down, put his hands on my shoulders, and looked into my eyes for a Power of Persuasion talk. "Brian, if you ever get to be an actor, don't get trapped into doing this shopping center nonsense. Six shows a day, six days a week, shocking pay, hot costumes. All actors want to work, but kickboxing zombies isn't exactly Hamlet, is it?"

"Don't you like being in *Zombie Squad*?" I asked. "I mean, you must get paid loads of money."

"You're kidding!" said Storm. "This show is the pits. We'd quit today, only we don't want to let down the kids. They are so into seeing their heroes. It's incredible how much they like *Zombie Squad*."

"Matthew likes it too much," I said. "It's kind of freaking him out."

"How's that?" asked Storm.

I told them. All about Matthew's sleepwalking, and about how he tried to beat up the old guy with the torn jacket, and about the bikers.

"Is Matthew going to watch today's show?" asked Ian the zombie.

"Not if I can stop him," I said. "He goes right off his rocker just watching it on TV. If he sees it live . . ." I started toward the door. "I have to find him."

Ian the zombie beckoned me back. "I've got a better idea." He winked at Storm. "What do you think, Geoff? Time for our special show?"

"What special show?" I asked.

"*Zombie Squad* is complete baloney," said Geoff. "It's just a clone of other kids' TV shows where cool young heroes solve the world's problems by bashing people. I mean, what sort of message is that sending to young kids?"

"It pretends to be all about teaching values—good and evil, saving the environment, that kind of stuff," said Ian the zombie. "But really it's just a way to sell merchandise. The same boring story over and over, always ending with the Z Squad heroes kickboxing their way out of trouble. If they tried that in the real world they'd all be locked up, and quite right, too."

"We've been joking for a while about how we could change the script of Z *Squad Live* to something more politically correct," said Storm. "Peace, love, and understanding, you know, and dropping the violence. But none of us are writers."

I took a deep breath. "I'm a writer," I said.

The show was starting in half an hour. There wasn't time to write a whole new play and have the actors learn it. Instead, we swapped a few ideas and Ian jotted them down on a roll of toilet paper.

"I like this, Ian," said Geoff. "I like it a lot. We'll let the others in on the plan and we can improvise the new bits. Don't miss the show, Brian."

Miss the show? No way! I couldn't wait for the show, to see what effect it had on Matthew.

improvisation *n.* im-pro-vy-zay-shun. Not having a clue what to do next, so you just make something up as you go along, and hope it might work out okay.

"Z SQUAD, dee-da-dum dee daa, Z Squad, dumm-ditty-daa-daa, Zombie Squad, da-da-daaaaaaaaaaaaaaa . . . dee dum!"

Colored lights flashed. Smoke filled the little stage set up in front of Woolfields. Hundreds of little voices cheered and screamed as Storm, Mitzi, and Big Boy cartwheeled out from behind a curtain.

I pulled Vince back into cover behind a pot of thick palms. Partly because I didn't want anyone to see me, and partly because I was now a playwright and could hardly bear the tension of watching my first play being acted out on stage.

It would take a while before the actors started on the new bits of the show that I'd suggested.

Z Squad Live started with a song:

> "We are Z Squad, hip hooray,
> While you go to school and play
> We make the world free
> Can't you see
> We kill zombies every day!"

They danced around doing kickboxing moves, and Big Boy showed the flying bottom drop he uses to squash zombies flat. The kids in the audience thought it was the funniest thing they'd ever seen. So did Dad—I spotted him now, at the back of the audience across from me. He was nodding away in

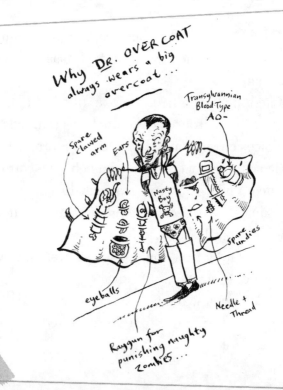

Why DR. OVERCOAT always wears a big overcoat...

Spare clawed arm

Ears

Transylvannian Blood Type A0-

Nasty Boy

Spare urdies

eyeballs

Needle + Thread

Raygun for punishing naughty zombies...

time with the music, a huge grin on his face. Next to him was Mom, leaning on a full shopping cart. Mom wasn't grinning. Neither one of them was looking in my direction.

When the song ended, Z Squad danced off stage, and Ian, Dr. Overcoat, and another zombie marched on. The kids in the audience booed and screamed, and two little girls in the front burst into tears and pushed their way back through the crowd to find their mommies.

Dr. Overcoat sang an evil song, while Ian and the other zombie did an evil dance behind him.

"Ha ha ha, hee hee hee,
I'll destroy ze world you see,
Z Squad are all sissies
and they can't stop me,
'Cause I'm an evil genius,
I'm mean and I'm bad
When zombies rule ze Earth,
I'll be really, really glad."

The shocking song finished and Dr. Overcoat ordered the zombies to go out into the streets of Garunga and destroy the environment. "Yes, ma-ster, we ob-ey!' chanted the zombies, and they walked stiffly back behind the curtain.

Then the Z Squad theme music blared out again, and Storm, Mitzi, and Big Boy bounded back on stage.

"Are those evil zombies planning something bad?" Storm asked the audience.

"Yeeeessss!" screamed three hundred five-year-olds.

"We'll have to put a stop to that. Won't we, boys and girls?" said Storm.

"Yeeeessss!" screamed the little voices again.

"And how will we stop the zombies?" asked Mitzi.

There was a pause while three hundred young brains tried to think of the possibilities.

Then a squeaky little voice cut through the air like Mitzi's whip. "Bash them!" screamed Matthew. I could see him now, watching through the bars of the balcony above the stage. Kelvin, Arthur, and Rocco were lined up behind him.

"How will we stop the zombies?" asked Storm.

"Bash them!" screamed the other kids in the crowd.

"Kill the zombies!" screamed Matthew. "Kill them now!"

Mom whispered something to Dad. He nodded and backed away toward the stairs.

The music stopped.

Storm stepped forward to the front of the stage and held up his arms.

"Just a minute, kids," he said. "Let's think this through. There are cleverer ways to deal with Dr. Overcoat."

This was the new part of the show I'd discussed with Geoff and Ian. From now on, Z *Squad Live* was going to get very interesting.

Dr. Overcoat whipped back the curtain and strode onto the stage. "Hee hee! You think you can defeat Dr. Overcoat? Think again, Z Squad!"

In the old show, this was where Storm did a couple of flips and kicked Dr. Overcoat in the chest. Instead, they began to act out the new lines I'd suggested to them.

Storm held up a little jar. "Dr. Overcoat, do you remember training these intelligent fleas?"

"My most brilliant scheme effer!" said Dr. Overcoat. "Clever fleas, trained to bite delegates at the Global Environment conference. They'll be too busy scratching to save the earth."

I'd read this story in Lancelot Cummins' book *Z Squad Itch for Action*. And I knew how Z Squad dealt with the situation . . .

"We'll see about that," said Storm. "We captured your fleas, and all the kids in town helped us to retrain them. Now they will only attack people . . . who have beards and overcoats!"

He whipped the lid off the jar and tipped it over Dr. Overcoat's head.

Dr. Overcoat screamed, "Not my mutant fleas! Zee biting! Zee itching! I cannot stand it!" He danced around the stage, scratching himself furiously, while the kids in the audience howled with laughter. Lancelot Cummins would have loved it. This was exactly the way it happened in the book, and it was much more fun than kickboxing!

Then Ian and the other zombie staggered onto the stage. "Z Squad-have-made-our lead-er itch-y!" they chanted. "Z-Squad-must-die!"

Storm and Mitzi and Big Boy backed away, pretending to be terrified. Then Storm said, "Let's see how tough these zombies are."

Mitzi said, "I've got my whip!"

Big Boy said, "I've got my big bottom ready to splatter them."

But Storm unrolled a roll of toilet paper and started reading a speech he and Ian the zombie had worked out. "Hold it right there, Z Squad. Bashing people you don't like doesn't solve anything. If we do that, it makes us zombie fighters just as bad and violent as our evil enemies."

"That is so true, Storm," said Mitzi. "Zombies are people, too, or at least, they're people who used to be people once. It's not the killer zombies' fault that they're undead. If we get to know them better, I'm sure we'll find that deep down they're really kind, and decent, too."

"Mitzi, you are so right," chimed in Big Boy, reading from his toilet paper roll. "Just because somebody eats live guinea pigs for breakfast doesn't mean they don't have feelings. I'm not going to sit on a zombie and splatter him ever again."

The kids in the audience stopped screaming and looked at each other, puzzled. This wasn't the way Z Squad heroes usually talked.

Storm said, "It's agreed then. From now on, we'll be nice to the zombies." Z Squad placed their fists one on top of another and shouted, "Be nice to zombies!"

Ian and the other zombie staggered around stiffly. "Des-troy Gar-unga! Des-troy Gar-unga!" they chanted.

Storm and Mitzi cartwheeled across the stage to block the zombies' path. "Hold it there, zombies!" said Storm.

Ian chanted, "Zom-bies must eat. Z Squad must die! Must have blood. Must have blood."

Big Boy and Mitzi held up two small boxes, with straws poking out of the end of them. Squeezee packs. "Hey zombies, like a Squeezee?"

"Yes, pleasee! Yes, pleasee!" chanted the zombies.

Dad had reached the balcony now and was edging his way through the crowd toward Matthew. At the mention of Squeezees he stopped and watched the show, too.

The zombies each took a Squeezee pack and sucked on the straw. They smiled and gave each other thumbs-up signs.

"Bet-ter than blood! Bet-ter than blood!" said one zombie.

"What is this ma-gic li-quid, zom-bie fight-er?" asked zombie Ian.

"It's a Squeezee," said Storm. He read the side of the packet. "It contains vitamins and minerals and is made from natural fruit ingredients, which kids and zombies need to build strong healthy bodies."

"Squee-zee good. Squee-zee good," said the other zombie.

Ian stepped forward and gave each of the three Z Squad fighters a big hug. With tears in his eyes, he said, "Thank you, Z Squad. Nobody has ever been kind to me before. All my life, and all my death, too, everybody treated me mean because I was an ugly killer zombie. Humans were afraid of me, because I looked different from them. They hated my red eyes and these scars on my cheeks.

"For the first time, you humans have shown me kindness and shared your delicious Squeezees with me. Now I know I was wrong to try to destroy the planet." He turned to the front of the stage. "This is a beautiful world we live in, children, and we should all be sharing it together. From now on, zombies and people will live in peace."

Storm said to the audience, "So boys and girls, next time we meet someone who looks a bit different from us, who has torn clothes, or speaks another language, maybe someone who comes from another country far away, or even someone we think might be a killer zombie, we don't have to be afraid of them, do we?"

"No!" called the three hundred five-year-olds.

"What will we do next time we meet a zombie?" asked Mitzi.

There was a pause. Her question hung in the air. The kids in the audience hoped they'd never meet a

zombie and have to make such a tricky decision. Then the silence was broken.

"Bash him!" screamed Matthew.

"Yessssss!" screamed the other little kids.

"Kill the zombies!" screamed Matthew. He climbed onto the railing. Kelvin Moray reached out to hold him, but he flattened Kelvin with a vicious back kick into his chest.

Mom screamed. "Matthew!" yelled Dad. But they were too late. Matthew jumped. He hit the heavy curtain at the back of the stage and slid down it. It collapsed under his weight, crumpling gently to the stage, giving him a soft landing in a mass of material. It also exposed Dr. Overcoat, who was sitting on a chair behind the stage, drinking a cup of coffee as he waited for his next entrance.

"Now you die!" yelled Matthew and threw himself at Dr. Overcoat.

Ian and the other zombie rushed to pull Matthew back, but when they saw a little boy being lifted up by two fierce zombies, other kids in the audience all surged forward to the stage, repeating, "Kill the zombies! Kill the zombies!"

The Z Squad actors tried to hold them back, but they were pushed aside. Little hands grabbed Ian by the ankle. He tried to shake himself free, but he had to be careful not to hurt any of the kids or kick anyone in the face. He fell, and little bodies piled on top of him.

It was chaos. The stage was surrounded by little faces contorted with hate, screaming, "Kill them, kill them, kill them!"

I tried to push toward the stage myself, but there was no way I could get through the crowd. I had to turn back. Then I saw one little face that wasn't screaming. Sebastian Chubb was watching in horror, holding hands with his sister, Madeline, who was thoughtfully munching a Nutter Butter cookie.

"Hello, Brian," yelled Madeline. "That was a really strange show, wasn't it? They should stop the riot though, or someone will get hurt."

"Nobody can stop it!" I yelled over the deafening screaming of hundreds of little voices.

"Yes, they could," yelled Madeline. Then she yelled a lot more stuff that I couldn't hear.

"What?" I yelled.

Madeline Chubb put her mouth to my ear and gave me a blast of Nutter Butter fumes, with crumbs added for emphasis. She pointed up to the ceiling of the shopping center.

"That's the craziest idea I ever heard in my life!" I yelled back. "No way am I doing that!"

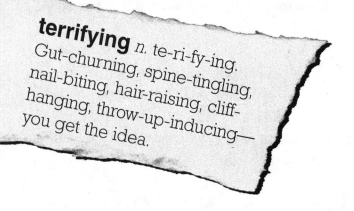

terrifying *n.* te-ri-fy-ing.
Gut-churning, spine-tingling, nail-biting, hair-raising, cliff-hanging, throw-up-inducing—you get the idea.

THERE are two things in life I'm exceptionally scared of: (1) heights—you know about that from earlier in the story—and (2) making myself look stupid. Now I was combining my two worst fears in one totally ridiculous freaky adventure.

I adjusted the garland of flowers around my head. "You look lovely, Brian," said Sebastian.

"Thanks, Sebastian." I didn't think I looked lovely at all. I looked totally, utterly, mind-bogglingly ridiculous. I was dressed as a fairy, in Sebastian's spare set of cellophane wings.

"Ooh, we're up really, really high, Brian," said Sebastian. We were on the very top balcony of Garunga Mall. The distance to the ground had to be at least 17,000,000 miles.

"Whatever you do, don't look down," I told him.

My voice was cool, calm, and controlled. I took a confidence-boosting puff on my asthma inhaler and sneaked a look over the edge of the balcony. Way, way below us, the tiny figures of Storm, Mitzi, and the zombies were fighting for their lives amid a heaving mass of yelling Z Squad fans. Somewhere in the crush was Matthew, but I couldn't see him.

There was a cleaners' platform tied up just below the balcony, dangling from a rope-and-pulley system from the ceiling of the building. The cleaners hadn't bothered to put it out of the reach of children. No children would ever come up to the top floor of Garunga Mall. There were no shops up here, only Ken Coalshutt and Associates Chartered Accountants, D.J. Solutions, and Center Administration.

"Hold on, Sebastian," I said. "Shut your eyes if you have to. Scream if you want to."

I stepped onto the platform. It dipped and swung and the ropes holding it up to the ceiling creaked. Sebastian reached out his arms to me. It was touching how much faith he had in his big buddy. It was a good thing he didn't know how scared I was.

Deep breath in. Deep breath out. "Go, Madeline!" I called.

Madeline Chubb pushed the platform away from the railing and wound the handle that controlled the rope-and-pulley system. The platform dropped into space. I screamed. Madeline pulled on the brake and we jerked to a stop.

Great Moments in Literature
By B. Hobble

ERIC   Mitzi

from "Z SQUAD'S GREAT ESCAPE" By L. Cummin

"Sorry," said Madeline, "I've never worked one of these before." She wound the handle again, more carefully this time, and the platform lowered us down . . . and down . . . and down . . . until we were exactly above the stage, level with the lower balcony.

"Look! It's The Kid Who Sucks!" called Mitzi. Parents stopped trying to yell over the screams of their kids. People began looking up and pointing and telling each other that something very interesting was happening right above their heads.

My fear of heights was replaced by my fear of looking stupid. I did look really, exceptionally, world-class stupid. And hundreds of people were watching me. Mom, Dad, my friend Vince. Worse, there was Kelvin Moray and his gang. I knew they'd tell the whole school what I'd done and who I'd been with and what I'd been wearing at the time. I'd be tormented about this incident for the rest of my life. Brian Hobble was truly The Kid Who Sucks.

The nightmare kept getting worse still, because below me I now saw Cassie Wyman. She'd arrived just in time to see me make a complete, utter, total idiot of myself.

No wonder everyone was staring. Sebastian and I were a pretty spectacular sight. Two fairies, one big and blue-haired and the other small and blond. If I didn't fall and splatter to death, I'd die of embarrassment.

"Can we use the fairy dust now?" asked Sebastian.

"Give it the works, Sebastian!" I said.

Together we two fairies chanted:

> "Fairy dust, fairy dust,
> Sugar and spice,
> Make bad children
> Turn out nice."

We threw handfuls of sparkly powder into the air, letting it drift down over the kids, over the zombies, over Z Squad, over Matthew—I could see him now, crawling out from under Dr. Overcoat. Fairy dust glistened as it caught the bright stage lights, then floated gently to settle on the heads of everyone below. The effect was magical. One by one, little Z Squad fans stopped punching and karate chopping and kickboxing. Instead, they fluttered their fingers in the clouds of fairy dust and looked up at us above them. Some of them waved. The masses stopped swarming, the rioters stopped rioting. Garunga Mall went very quiet. Z *Squad Live* was over.

I gave a thumbs-up to Madeline above us. She wound the handle again, and the cleaners' platform slowly descended, gently lowering Sebastian and me toward the center of the stage.

Before it touched the ground, I jumped off and pulled Matthew to his feet. "Hello, Brian," he said. "You look funny."

Then everybody started to clap.

When things calmed down there was lots of hugging that I don't want to bore you with. I'll just give you the short version of it.

Mom cried and hugged Matthew. Dad hugged Matthew and me and crushed my fairy wings. Then Mom hugged Dad. Only for a moment, then they broke apart, looking a bit embarrassed and awkward.

I hugged Sebastian. Madeline Chubb raced down the escalators to hug Sebastian, too, and crushed his wings. Then she hugged me, too, and for some weird reason I hugged her back. Vince grabbed me around the neck and pressed his fist into the side of my face. I can't explain it—it's just something your friends do when they get excited.

Storm and Ian gave me high fives, Big Boy gave me a big sweaty bear hug, and Mitzi gave me a kiss. It wasn't quite like Tiffany's kiss, but I didn't mind being kissed by a spunky superhero in a blue wet suit.

Cassie hung back a bit. I tried to edge away and avoid catching her eye. No way would she want to talk to an overgrown fairy with crumpled wings. Especially not with all those Garunga kids watching. I'd totally blown my chances with her.

Cassie Wyman pushed past Madeline, put her hands on my shoulders, and stared the Power of Persuasion into my eyes. "Awesome, Brian!" she said. And she kissed me. It mostly missed my mouth, banged my nose, and some of her hair got caught up with it, too. She was in a rush, I suppose, and a bit flustered. There were people everywhere. She pulled away from me and muttered, "Sorry, Brian . . . I just sort of felt like doing that." Technically, I'd had better kisses. But I didn't feel the need to wipe it off. My head was spinning, and I was looking forward to doing take two sometime soon. With a bit of practice, we were sure to get it right.

Z Squad lined up to shake hands with Matthew. Then the zombies did the same. Dr. Overcoat stripped off his costume, so we could see what he was wearing underneath. A Green Planet T-shirt with a picture of a baby seal on it. "It's just a story, Matthew," he said. "You understand that, don't you?" Matthew nodded.

"There's no such thing as zombies, dude," said Ian. "Want to help me clean off my makeup?"

"No," said Matthew.

"Good decision, Matthew," said Big Boy. "Ian's face is even scarier without his makeup."

The actors all laughed. Just like Z Squad used to do at the end of each TV episode.

Then lots of people said they were sorry. Mom was sorry for not believing what I told her about Matthew and Z Squad. Dad was sorry for forcing me to do the Squeezee ad when I didn't want to. I said I didn't mind it too much, it was a useful life experience, and I sort of liked being The Kid Who Sucks. Dad said Sun River Fruits would be rethinking their sponsorship of *Zombie Squad*.

Then Matthew came over to me. "Gee, you look funny, Brian."

"I don't care," I said.

"You were really brave to go up that high, Brian."

"It wasn't really so dangerous," I said.

"But you're scared of heights, aren't you, Brian?" said Matthew. "I know 'cause I saw you up that tree with the dog." How had he noticed that? "So you were really, really, reeeeeeeally a hero to do that. Thank you for saving me. I was kind of crazy."

"That's okay," I said. I gave my little brother a hug, and he hugged me back.

Over his shoulder I saw Kelvin Moray and his gang walking away. I knew they'd tell the whole school about me dressing up as a fairy and scattering fairy dust. But I didn't care.

Sebastian hugged me, too, and I ruffled his hair. "You're a great little buddy, Sebastian. Sometimes it's really useful to have a fairy companion. You wear those wings any time you want to, and if people say dumb things, just take no notice."

Sebastian reached up and laid his hands on both my shoulders. He stared deep into my eyes. "Fairies is only a game, Brian. Fairies aren't real."

"No, of course they're not, Sebastian." (*The Truth Machine gives a little blip. Ouch!*)

Maybe the fairy act worked just by distracting the people who were going crazy, and making them watch someone else make a complete and utter idiot of himself. Maybe there really was something special about fairy dust. I'd never know for sure. I hoped I wouldn't need to try it ever again.

Cool moves on Rollerblades
by B. HOBBLE
N° ② The Banister Slide

epilogue *n*. epi-log. Bit at the end of a book after the exciting action is all over, so you're not sure whether to put it in or leave it out.

TO: Brian.Hobble@supernet.com
FROM: Lancelot_Cummins@lancelotcummins.com
SUBJECT: Well done again!

Dear Brian,

Thank you for sending me your "Freaky Stuff" story. Plenty of action, lots of fun, and I enjoyed reading it very much.

Brian, you certainly have a very vivid imagination. Everybody does, of course, but I'm delighted to see you have the perseverance to write down the odd ideas that pop up inside your head. Not enough young people take the trouble to do that.

Keep on writing, and I look forward to seeing more of your inventive stories as you make them up.

Lance

P.S. Was that really *you* in the Squeezee ad on TV? I don't remember you having blue hair.

TO: Lancelot_Cummins@lancelotcummins.com
FROM: Brian.Hobble@supernet.com
SUBJECT: RE: Well done again!

Dear Lance,

Yes, it is me in the ad. The blue has grown out of my
hair now, which is good, 'cause now people don't say

"Like a Squeezee?" to me all the time. I was famous for a while, but I'm glad it's over, and I'm just The Kid Who Used to Suck. Next time I get famous I want to be famous like you, and not have people recognize me.

By the way, I'm sorry they've taken *Zombie Squad* off TV.

Sun River Fruits is sponsoring this new show, and my little brother, Matthew, and his best friend, Sebastian Chubb, watch it at our place every day. It's about a pixie called Twinkletoes, who sprinkles fairy dust and helps out at tea parties. It's called *Fairy Magic* and it's freaky how popular it is. Every kid in Garunga Elementary School has a *Fairy Magic* backpack, even Matthew's got a wand and wings. Kids my age are into *Fairy Magic*, too. Abby and Sarah and Sofie wear flower headbands to school.

You wouldn't believe it, Lance, but suddenly the coolest, trendiest kid in Garunga District School is Sebastian Chubb.

Your fan,

Brian Hobble

TO: Brian.Hobble@supernet.com
FROM: Lancelot_Cummins@lancelotcummins.com
SUBJECT: Zombie Squad

Dear Brian,

I don't mind that *Zombie Squad* isn't on TV anymore.

As you know, I wasn't all that happy with the treatment of the stories.

Another producer hopes to turn my book *Nose Job* into a film soon, starring a young actor named Chadley Stevens—have you heard of him? I'm writing the *Nose Job* script myself, so I hope to have more control. So no kickboxing I'm afraid, but it will still be disgusting, funny, and action packed—the sort of thing kids like you enjoy!

Best wishes,

Lancelot Cummins

P.S. Are you writing another story yourself?

THE HIGH-Life of
BRIAN
veronica Lovelace
(the rise of a great man)

Starring Cassie
the Beautiful

R

My future Career
Highlights

By B. HOBBLE

Nº ① A Series of Romance/Adventure novels inspired by ME !!

TO: Lancelot_Cummins@lancelotcummins.com
FROM: Brian.Hobble@supernet.com
SUBJECT: My next story

Dear Lance,

I'm making a picture book for my little buddy. My friend comes around here on the days when I'm looking after Matthew, and we work on it together. Most days we talk more than we write, so it might take a long time to finish the book. I don't care if it takes a megasquintillion years, because the friend is Cassie Wyman.

Got to go, Lance. She's just arrived.

See you,

Brian

The End

The End

thank yous *n.* than-kewz. Nice things to say about people who help you.

Thank you, Eva Mills and the team at Random House for your early faith in Brian Hobble and your continuing encouragement as he fumbles around, learning to write his stories. Thanks again, Melissa Balfour for the great editing suggestions and for trying to stop me getting away with sloppy, slovenly, slapdash work. Brian would hate rewriting his stories, but they're always better when you've made him do it! Thank you to my family, and to the teachers and kids who listened to me reading bits of *Freaky Stuff* when I visited your schools. You helped me work out what to keep in the story and which totally boring bits to ditch, toss, reject, discard, and chuck out.

R.T.